TALES
FROM THE
PARK
LAND

RONALD MCGILLVRAY

To my wife, Martha, for her patience and g
To my son, James, who was my muse even if he
To my mom, Roberta, who took me to my firs

CONTENTS

THE GARBAGE COLLECTORS

The bus pulled up to my stop so I got off and began my short walk home. The same neighbors who'd ignored me in the morning were all smiles and waves as I passed by. I waved back and smiled but didn't stop to chat. I'd commented to my wife a few days earlier how strange our neighbors seemed but she told me it was all in my imagination. I crossed the street and couldn't help but stare at the house that I'd dreamt about the night before. Just thinking about it caused me to shudder. In front of the house sat a van crammed with boxes and small tables. More furniture was piled on its roof. It looked like they were moving. I thought back on my dream as if it might have been a premonition. Nah, they must have been planning the move beforehand. I was still thinking about the incident when I walked in my front door.

"Stephen, can you come in here please?" my wife Sarah called from the family room.

What now?

"Patrick's upstairs crying and won't come out of his room." She had a worried look on her face and she was fidgeting with some framed pictures on a shelf. Never a good sign.

"What's the matter? Is he sick?"

"No, something happened at school. I think some kids picked on him but I can't get the whole story out of him."

"Was he hurt?"

"No, I don't think it was anything physical. Can you try talking to him?" she asked, looking more than desperate.

"Sure. I'll go up there right now. It'll be fine," I said trying to assure her.

I placed my briefcase against the wall and walked towards the stairs. As I passed my wife, I stopped for a second to kiss her. I got the smile I was looking for and headed up the stairs.

I heard sobbing from the other side of Patrick's door. I knocked a few times before I finally let myself in. Patrick was lying on his bed his head facing the wall. He looked up briefly and I could see he'd been crying for a while. His eyes were puffy and red and he looked like he'd been through the wringer.

"What a terrible day I had at work," I said, trying to commiserate with my son. "Looks like you had a bad one too. Want to come downstairs with me and have a beer so we can talk about it?"

That got a bit of a grin but the sobbing started again. Without warning, Patrick jumped off his bed, ran over to me and wrapped his arms around me.

"Whoa there little buddy, what's the matter?"

"You wouldn't let anyone take me away would you, Daddy?"

"What are you talking about? Of course not. Who'd help me with the chores?" I tried to make a joke of it but what he'd said had put a knot in my stomach.

"Some of the kids at school told me the garbage collectors were going to come and get me and there was nothing you could do about it," Patrick managed between sniffles.

"Garbage collectors? What are you talking about? Do you look like garbage?" I asked, putting on my best daddy-knows-best smile.

"These are a different kind of garbage collectors," he said as tears welled up in his eyes.

"Okay, you'd better tell me the whole story from the beginning."

Patrick seemed hesitant at first but then opened up, letting it all come flowing out. "Kids at school told me that on the night before garbage day, the garbage collectors come out and hunt through peoples' garbage. They look for a sign that'll tell them which kid will be next to go to the dump." Patrick took a deep breath.

"Oh really? And what happens to these kids who end up at the dump?"

"They're eaten by the garbage collectors. It's what keeps the garbage collectors alive."

"I see. Don't you think the parents might have something to say about it?"

"The parents are the ones who give the kids to the garbage collectors," he said, tears streaming down his face. "If the garbage collectors come, can you give them Kim instead of me? I promise I'll be good and do everything you guys say."

I felt the knot move from my stomach up to my throat. The feeling of rage which I knew so well stirred inside of me like fire. I wanted to go find these kids and give them something to really be afraid of, but I'd worked hard at keeping my temper under control and I wasn't going to blow all that hard work now.

"Don't worry, I have no plans to let either you or Kim end up at the dump."

"Promise?" Patrick asked, looking at me with pleading eyes.

"Yes, I promise," I answered. "So, are these kids sent away because they were bad?"

"No, the families do it to save their other boy or girl."

"What if the family only has one child?" I asked not so innocently, hoping to poke holes in the story.

"No one does here. Everyone in town has two kids. Haven't you noticed?" He stopped for a moment to catch his breath. "Danny told me, they only let you live here if you come with two."

What imagination kids have these days, I mused. Then I asked, "Why wouldn't the parents just pack up and leave if they found out about this?"

"We can't leave. There's no way out of here," Patrick answered, with all the conviction he could muster.

"Well, we came here from somewhere, didn't we?"

"Yes."

"So, if we came here from somewhere, we can always go back there, right?"

"I suppose," he answered.

"There you have it."

"But they said people have tried to leave before and have always ended up coming back."

"That's just nonsense. In fact, I just saw the people about eight houses down all packed and ready to move. Where do you think they're going?"

"That's the Donnelley's. They have to give up their son tonight."

"The other kids tell you that?"

"Yes," Patrick answered.

"Well, if these kids know so much, did they tell you what these garbage collectors look like?"

"They're like shadows. They're all black and hate the light. They have big glowing eyes," he answered, tears once again welling up in his eyes.

I felt a cold sweat form on my back as I recalled the strange dream I'd had last night. I'd been looking out one of the bedroom windows when I noticed what I thought was just a shadow across the road. But hadn't the shadow looked like it had been going through the garbage? Then out of the corner of my eye, I'd noticed another black figure glide across the street to join it. I'd watched them as they inspected the neighbor's garbage unaware someone was watching them. Suddenly, one of them turned to face me and I'd tripped over myself, landing on my ass. I'd slowly picked myself up and looked back out the window towards where the dark figures had been but they were gone. Several crows pecked away at the garbage instead. As I'd turned away, a movement had caught my eye, and when I turned back, a dark figure sat crouched on my garage roof, staring directly at me.

I had woken up drenched in sweat and immediately went to check on the kids.

I thought about the dream for a moment until an idea popped into my head. "Go get your shoes and your sister, we're going for a drive. I'll get Mom."

"Where are we going?" Patrick asked, between sniffles.

"I am going to prove to you that we can drive out of this town any time we want," I answered.

A sudden look of relief washed over my son's face as he hurried into his closet to grab his shoes, calling out for Kim at the same time. I went back downstairs.

"What's going on?" Sarah asked. "How's Patrick?"

"I think he'll be all right," I told her. "Some kids told him a story and it had him spooked. So, we're going to go for a ride in the car to make him feel better."

Sarah looked at me strangely but grabbed her purse as Kim came down the stairs with Patrick right behind her.

"Okay, are we ready?" I asked.

"Where are we going?" Kim asked.

"We're going out for dinner to a restaurant this evening."

"Which restaurant?"

4

"The first restaurant we come to outside the city limits. I'm going to prove something to your brother."

"Let me guess. He told you we can't get out of here, right?"

Her comment stopped me cold and I looked at her in surprise.

"Why do you say that?" I asked.

"I heard the same story today at school. They told me I'd never be able to leave the city and there was some evil force at work here."

"Who told you that? Did you overhear Patrick and I talking?"

"No, I didn't hear you guys talking. Some losers in my class told me. There's a group of them who think they know it all, but they're nothing but brainless hicks."

"Well I have to agree with your description of the locals so far," I laughed.

"Stephen!" Sarah cautioned me.

"It's true, honey. The neighbors haven't exactly been welcoming."

"Maybe we should give them the benefit of the doubt," she suggested.

"Sure, whatever. I'm just venting."

"Okay enough of this," Sarah said. "Let's get going. I can't remember the last time your father offered to take us out, so we'd better get going before he changes his mind."

Everyone laughed as we headed out the door and piled into the car. I put the key into the ignition and started it up. "So far so good," I said with a big grin.

"Just drive," the three of them said in unison.

I backed the car out of the driveway and followed the tree-lined street to the first stop sign and turned right. I followed a winding road until we came to a major intersection. Sarah spotted the sign to the highway first and pointed it out. I made a quick couple of lane changes until finally we were on the highway.

"Here we are then. Well on our way and no problems so far," I said, more to Patrick than anyone else. "So tell me, Kim. What else did you hear about this place?" I asked, as I pulled into the far-right lane and settled in for the ride.

"It's just a bunch of nonsense," she replied.

"Humor me."

"Fine," she answered, exasperated, "Alison Crimble said there are things living in or around the garbage dump. I can't remember which."

"Go on," I prodded.

"Anyway, supposedly the dump is on some old forgotten burial site. The things buried there feed off the life force of children," she said, as she rolled her eyes.

"And do you believe the story?" I asked.

"Of course not, duh."

"See Patrick, your sister doesn't believe the story."

Patrick didn't say a word but continued to stare out the window at the passing trees. The car was silent as we continued to drive down the highway. The sun was still bright in the sky even though it was closing in on seven o'clock. The sound of the wheels on the road gave off a hypnotic hum. I looked over at Sarah and she seemed to be daydreaming. I took a peek in the rearview mirror and saw Kim sitting with her usual scowl. Patrick though seemed to be studying the outside landscape for something I couldn't fathom. Seeing this little trip wasn't helping my son the way I'd planned, I decided to strike the conversation back up.

"How do these things manage to find the children they want?"

"Well supposedly, they go through the garbage at night and look for personal items. That's how they decide who they're going to pick."

"Going to pick?" I asked.

"Yeah, when they find the item they're looking for they leave a mark or something, letting the family know they've been chosen to give up one of their children."

"I see," I said with a smirk, looking at Sarah who didn't seem to find any of this amusing. "What if the family only has one child?"

"That's the only thing that spooked me. It seems everyone at school has either a brother or a sister. There doesn't seem to be any families with just one kid around here."

Once again, the car became silent.

"Shouldn't we have reached an exit ramp by now?" Sarah asked, breaking the silence.

"Not sure," I answered. "I got caught up in the story and wasn't keeping an eye out."

"Well, it's starting to get late and the kids are probably hungry. Let's find a place soon, okay?"

"Sure, no problem. Once we cross the city limit there's a restaurant on the other side of the highway. I remember seeing it when we first arrived."

"Who would you pick?" Patrick asked out of the blue.

"What?" Sarah and I said at the same time.

"Who would you pick? You know if they came to our house and left their mark."

"It's just a story," I answered, beginning to feel exasperated.

"But just for fun, if you had to choose, which one of us would you send away?"

"The one who asked too many stupid questions."

"Stephen," Sarah scolded. "Daddy didn't mean that, he was just trying to be funny."

"Well, I'm serious," Patrick said. "I want to know. Which of us would you pick?"

"Yeah Dad, which of us would you send to the monsters?" Kim piped in.

"Now they're monsters, eh? I thought they were garbage collectors."

"Funny Dad," Kim said without a smile.

"Look you two, it's just a story. But for the sake of an argument, if it was true, I would refuse to give either of you up."

"Supposedly you don't have a choice," Patrick said. "One of the kids in my class told me a family tried that once and barricaded themselves in their house."

"And what happened?" I asked, keeping an eye on the road.

"The neighbors made the choice. They broke down the door and took one of the kids to the dump themselves."

"Is that what you heard, Kim?"

"Yeah, Dad," she said. "It's just a stupid story, right?"

"Of course, Pumpkin."

"You know something, Stephen?" Sarah said. "I know we've only been here around a week but now that I think about it, everyone I've met so far has two kids."

"Not you too."

"Don't you find it strange?"

"You're not helping the matter here, Hon. Have you seen any signs for an exit yet?"

"No, I haven't," she answered. "The sun's already starting to set and we should have hit the city limits a long time ago."

"Maybe we missed it when we were all talking," I suggested, trying to sound optimistic.

"Patrick," Sarah asked suddenly. "What happens to the child who's left behind?"

"Sarah." It was my turn to be indignant.

"It's okay Dad," Patrick said. "The kid that's left is given some sort of special powers."

"And what is this special power?" I asked, no longer hiding the fact I was getting tired of all this nonsense.

"They wouldn't tell me," Patrick answered.

"What about you Kim?" I tried again.

"Same thing. They wouldn't tell me, but they said it's worth it and the family goes away to a wonderful place."

"A wonderful place, eh?" I muttered, tapping the steering wheel in agitation.

"Yeah, to make room for a new family," Kim added. "That's why you never see a family with only one kid."

"Jesus Stephen, step on the gas and get us out of here. This whole thing is starting to freak me out," Sarah pleaded.

I accelerated and took another look into the rearview mirror only to see the heartbreaking sight of my son crying quietly in the backseat. Rage began to flow through me again like a freight train. I couldn't recall feeling like this for some time. I'd battled with my anger management problems before and beaten them, so what the hell was wrong with me now? And where was the damn restaurant?

The sun now sat well below the tree line and I was sure we should have been well past the city limits by now, but the highway seemed to just go on and on. There weren't even any bends in the road anymore, just straight highway as far as the eye could see. Once again the car fell silent and I wondered what everyone was thinking. The fact I couldn't reassure them that everything was going to be okay drove me crazy, but not half as much as the thought that all this might be true.

We'd been driving for hours and nothing in the scenery had changed. There were no other cars on the road either. Sarah had stopped badgering me to turn around and sat in her seat mute, gazing out the window at seemingly the same trees we'd been passing for hours. Both Patrick and Kim were asleep in the backseat. What the hell was going on?

I felt like I was going to be sick, but there was no way I'd go see that therapist again. The thought of it got me even more upset.

"Sarah?" I asked, needing the comfort of another voice.

"Yes," she answered.

"Do you want me to turn around?"

"I want you to tell me what's happening," she said, with tears in her eyes. She looked into the backseat at the loves of her life.

"I have no answers," I answered. "I'm sorry."

"This can't be happening. This is all just some mistake, right?"

"I just don't know anymore," I replied.

"Then let's just go back. We're not getting anywhere. Besides, once we get home, we can call someone outside the city for help."

"And what are we going to say?" I asked, sounding a bit more sarcastic than I'd meant.

"Let's just go home," she said.

I slowed the car down and looked at the dashboard clock. It was past eleven o'clock. My God, we'd been driving for almost five hours. This was madness. I did a quick shoulder check and turned the car around, heading back into town. My eyes felt heavy and I wondered if I'd be able to make it back without falling asleep at the wheel. As I drove along the dark deserted highway, I tried to find flaws in the stories the kids had told but with what we'd experienced so far, I couldn't. I thought about my office co-workers and how they all seemed like good, decent people. I couldn't see any of them buying into this crap. I pictured each individual I'd met at the office and recalled how they'd all spoken with love when it came to their children.

The memory hit me like a tidal wave. Everyone I'd spoken with had shown me pictures of their two kids.

Two kids.

Just as my eyes started to close from exhaustion, I spotted lights ahead. I glanced at the dashboard clock again and saw we'd only been driving for about ten minutes in this direction. How come we hadn't noticed the lights earlier? I focused on the lights as we drove towards them.

I looked over at Sarah, but she was asleep. I decided to wait until we reached the restaurant before I woke them. I couldn't believe I'd started to buy into the kids' stories. I let out a little chuckle. I drove into the lit area and my smile turned to a grimace of horror when I recognized where we were. We hadn't found the exit at all. We were back in the town we'd been trying to escape. I looked back at the dashboard clock and calculated the drive which took almost five hours one way took only fifteen minutes on the way back. I wanted to scream in frustration but held it in for the sake of my family. I looked over at Sarah beside me and at my two precious children who were asleep and felt lost.

I exited the highway and found myself on Main Street. I followed it through town, passing businesses and restaurants. As I drove along, everything looked and seemed so normal. What was I expecting, I wondered? Should there be people in the streets wearing Druid costumes or something more fitting for a city that gave up their own?

I saw the sign I'd been looking for and turned left. I followed the road until it turned to dirt and continued on. I had a purpose now because I had just remembered that today was garbage day.

I followed the dirt road which became bumpier the further I drove. The road led into a dense forest, the trees were close to the road and seemed to grab out at the car as it passed by. Visibility became worse. Maybe this wasn't such a great idea. I looked around at my family but they were still asleep, so I kept driving.

Finally, I saw a clearing ahead. I slowed down and took another look at the dashboard clock. It was a few minutes before midnight. There was a bend in the road ahead, so I slowed down. In the glimmer of the headlights, I saw the sign.

Town Dump.

I stopped the car to stare at it for a moment then continued around the bend.

There it was.

A fiery glow from behind one of the mounds of trash lit up the area around it. I saw movement ahead and squinted my eyes in an attempt to see better. In the soft light of the dump's eerie glow, I spotted the woman who lived in the house where the packed van had sat this morning. I didn't think she'd noticed me yet, so I turned off the headlights and drove closer. She wasn't alone. Her husband was there as well, and they were both looking at something on the other side of the fence.

"Oh my God," I whispered in horror, following their gaze.

Inside the dump's compound, a young boy around the same age as Patrick stared through the fence. The boy faced his parents, rattling the gates, trying desperately to get out.

Through the car window, I could hear the boy crying and pleading with the couple to let him out. The woman cried as well but the man held her firm. I watched the boy beg for his parents' help while turning his head around constantly as if to see if something was coming up behind him.

I wasn't sure what to do. Instinctively I wanted to plow my car through the gate and rescue the boy. If I ran down the parents, so much the better. But I had my own family to think of. This whole thing was insane.

At that moment the fiery glow brightened, lighting almost the entire area. I couldn't take my eyes off the pleading boy who now shook the fence even harder. The boy was in a frenzy. He tried to climb the fence but was unable to manage it. Something else caught my eye. From behind the glowing mounds of garbage, dark figures had begun to emerge.

I watched in horror but dragged my eyes away to check on my own boy. When I looked back the young boy was trying desperately to dig under the fence with his fingers, always looking behind him.

To my shock I noticed the parents walking away, turning their backs on their own flesh and blood. I felt nauseous and my head began to spin. There were too many emotions going through me at once and I felt as if I were going to go mad.

The black figures closed in on the boy. He was back on his feet shaking the gate with both his little hands and calling out for his mother. A switch seemed to go off in my head and before I knew what I was doing, I had the headlights back on and the car speeding towards the gate. The boy started to run, the black ghouls closing in on him. Why hadn't I acted sooner? I continued to drive faster towards the gate at a good ramming speed.

As the gate got closer, the car's headlights lit the area ahead of me. I saw the terrified boy running as fast as his little legs could carry him over and around the garbage heaps, trying desperately to get away. The boy stumbled and before he could scramble back to his feet the black forms were on him. I took my foot off the gas pedal and let the car coast to a stop, I'd been too late. I pressed my head against the steering wheel and drew deep breaths. The image of the little boy was forever burned into my memory. I felt tears well up and I choked down the scream building up within me. Once again I was overcome with a myriad of emotions. But one emotion stormed to the top of the heap.

Rage.

I turned the car around and drove away trying desperately to work out a plan to protect my family. I spotted the parents of the little boy walking glumly along the side of the road, they didn't even turn when the headlights illuminated them. Just as well, I thought, as I gave the car a little gas and ran them down. I hated them for not warning me about the dump.

I hated them all.

I turned on the windshield wipers and gave a few quick bursts of windshield wiper fluid to clean off the splattered blood now covering the windshield.

I looked down at the dashboard clock. It was well after midnight.

"What's going on?" Sarah asked, startling me.

"Sorry, Hon. Did I wake you?"

"No, I think I was having a nightmare. Where are we?" she asked, still half asleep.

"While you were dozing, lazybones, I found our mysterious exit," I lied. "We must have passed it while we were telling our ghost stories. Everything's fine," I tried desperately to gain control of the rage I'd let loose.

"Why do you have the windshield wipers on," she asked. "Did it rain?"

"No, we hit an animal. It ran out from the woods, and I didn't see it in time."

"Are we almost home?" she asked as if she hadn't heard my last statement.

"Yep. I just wanted to go check out the dump first," I answered.

"The dump?" she repeated, still half asleep.

"Yeah, it's just a dump. Nothing unusual there. I just had to see for myself."

"And you found the city limit and the exit we were looking for?" she asked hopefully.

"Yes, and we can come and go from the city anytime we want. Just like I said."

That was all the reassurance she needed as she fell back into her interrupted sleep. I drove home and parked in the driveway. I nudged Sarah awake and then woke up the kids and got them safely into their beds.

"I guess I still owe you guys a dinner," I said with a smirk, as we walked into the bedroom.

"Don't worry, I'll remind you," she said, smiling back at me. She kissed me on the cheek. "Are you coming to bed?"

"In a bit. I just want to check out the front of the car and clean whatever blood's still on there. Don't want to freak out the kids tomorrow morning."

"Okay, don't stay up too late." Sarah got into bed. "Won't be long before you have to get up again."

"I'll be up soon." I walked over to the bed and gave her a soft kiss on the lips.

"What's that for?"

"Just for being the best wife a guy could have."

I stopped in the washroom where I threw some cold water on my face and took a good long look at myself. I wasn't sure I liked what I saw. I walked next to Kim's room and looked at her for a moment. I smiled and placed a gentle kiss on her forehead before going into Patrick's room and doing the same.

"Goodnight slugger," I said, and with tears in my eyes, I walked from the room.

I went downstairs and followed the back hallway past the laundry room to the garage door. I stood there for a minute before finally opening it and stepping into the garage. I turned the light on, crossed the garage, and began clearing a spot on my work-bench. I spotted the locked metal box I was looking for and carefully took it down from its resting place. I unlocked it with a key from my key ring and opened the box.

The revolver gleamed.

I took out 4 bullets, kissing each one of them before loading them into the gun.

I held the gun in my hands as I knelt and prayed, tears streaming down my face. Afterward, I stood up and slowly walked to the garage door that led into the house. I turned off the garage light, opened the door, and entered the house.

For the last time.

UBIQUITY

The warm air blew over James as his boat moved across the open water. It wasn't air-conditioning but at least it wasn't the hot stagnant air he had become accustomed to over the last week. As the mainland's shoreline drew closer, he noticed the lack of traffic along the usually busy waterfront.

James eased his boat in among the others moored there and again noticed the lack of activity.

He secured his boat and walked down the pier towards the office to pay his mooring charge. There was no one there except several crows that stood perched on the office roof staring intently at him.

"Hello?" he called out, as he entered the office.

No one answered.

After a quick look around, he exited the office and set out to find someone who could help him. He reached the main street which ran along the waterfront, usually busy with traffic and pedestrians, but saw no one. Where was everybody, he wondered? The quiet began to make him uneasy.

He left the waterfront and made his way inland towards the core of the city.

There were cars everywhere, all abandoned. He opened the door of one of them and noticed the keys were still in the ignition. It seemed the car had been left running and had simply run out of gas. He checked some other cars and found the same thing. A feeling of uneasiness had settled in.

He searched one street after another, looking for signs of life but found no one. He spotted a grocery store and walked towards it. The automatic doors wouldn't open. He pressed his face against the glass doors and noticed the lights inside were off. He pulled the doors open.

"Hello, anybody here?" he called out. He didn't receive an answer, so he walked further in and called out yet again.

Still no answer.

A strange feeling that he was being watched came over him and he decided he didn't want to stick around.

James spent the rest of the afternoon walking what seemed the entire length and width of the city but came across no one.

What the hell was going on and where the fuck was everybody?

He pressed on, desperate to find answers but night was approaching quickly.

The darkening sky hadn't diminished the uncomfortable heat, however. It was worse here in the city than on the island. He thought for a moment about heading back to the island but realized he'd better stick around and try to find out what was going on. As the sky continued to darken around him, he decided it might be time to find a place to hole up for the night.

He spotted the local headquarters of a major insurance company just up the street. He knew it was the tallest building in the city and if he could make it to the top, he'd have a bird's-eye view of the city below. He walked towards the building but as he crossed the street, the staccato sound of automatic gunfire filled the air. James raced to the closest building he saw. As he crashed through the front doors, he hit the ground. Slowly he crawled to a window and looked out.

For the moment all was quiet.

Another burst of automatic gunfire exploded in the evening air, followed by more silence.

The gunfire wasn't close, but they were close enough.

He lay motionless for a few moments listening.

When everything seemed safe, he crawled slowly to the front entrance and looked out into the dark street. He opened the door slowly, stopping to listen for anything unusual. He didn't hear anything but after some thought, he decided to stay put. He closed the door quietly and turned to look around at his surroundings. He laughed when he saw where he was. The huge chandelier that hung from the high ceiling gave it away. He was in the Grand Capital, the most elegant hotel in the city.

If you're going to be holed up somewhere, this would be the best place to do it, he thought. He took in the grand staircase and the luxurious furniture that surrounded him and began to feel much better about his situation.

Then it dawned on him the elevators wouldn't be working.

After an exhausting climb to the top of the hotel, he set himself up in his new digs after finding a master key still attached to a housekeeping cart.

The view from his suite was better than he could have hoped for. He would have been able to see all the way to the waterfront if it hadn't been so dark. He gazed across the city landscape wondering what had happened to everyone.

As he looked out over the darkening city, something across the street caught his eye. He searched for it, but it was too dark to make anything out.

Suddenly, from somewhere below, a searchlight lit up the building across the street, temporarily blinding him. He closed his eyes for a moment then looked across the way and couldn't believe his eyes. Clinging to the wall of the building, close to twenty floors up, was a man.

No, not a man but a creature.

Was he seeing right? The thing looked to have extra arms coming out of its side. Its head was much larger than a man's and its eyes were so huge they took up most of its forehead. The thing tried to protect its eyes by holding up one of its many hands in front of its face, somehow defying gravity. How could it stay attached to the wall, James wondered? It was like a human spider, some deformed creature from a B movie that you'd see on a double bill at a drive-in.

A burst of gunfire peppered the side of the building and the thing scurried away, dodging the bullets. James watched horrified as the gunfire increased and the thing tried to make its way to safety. It quickly disappeared over the top of the building, the searchlight following its path. James pulled the drapes closed.

Tired and feeling trapped, James lay down on the bed and cursed himself for leaving the island. Since taking up residence on the island, after the murder of his wife and daughter during a robbery at their home, he had sworn never to leave it. He had once been a prosperous attorney in the city but that had all changed in the blink of an eye one horrible night 3 years ago. Now he was living another nightmare. One that, like the other, he could not wake up from.

Shouting startled James from his thoughts. He instinctively rolled off the bed and listened closely to the commotion outside his room. He couldn't make out what was being said but he realized that it couldn't be good. He moved to the door and listened to what was going on out in the hallway. From what he could tell, doors were being kicked in and whoever it was out there was getting closer.

His brain raced with a multitude of ideas, none of them bearing fruit. He had nowhere to run and even fewer places to hide. The racket was only a few doors down now.

Who was out there? Friend or foe? Were they here to help or were they out to kill anyone or anything they found? Or worse, could it be those spider things? Had they somehow gotten into the building?

He raced back to the window, drew open the drapes, and screamed.

Looking at him through the window was one of those creatures. Its two large dark eyes stared directly at him. The thing opened its mouth and thick spittle drooled from it. James couldn't move. He felt like gagging and his chest grew tight as if someone was sitting on it. He noticed the thing's hands, which secreted a sticky substance against the window.

What the hell had happened while he was away on his island? The thing turned its head away for a moment as if something else had caught its attention but then quickly shot its gaze back at James.

The door to his room suddenly crashed in. A shotgun blast lit up the room and then another exploded by his head. He threw himself to the ground and rolled to the side of the bed as the window behind him blew out into the night.

The smell of gunpowder drifted through the room.

"Who's there? Show yourself?" a man's voice yelled.

James didn't budge, hoping whoever it was would go away. He could feel a breeze coming from the shattered window. Was the thing in the room?

"Show yourself," barked the voice again.

"Don't shoot. I'm unarmed," James called out.

"Show yourself. I won't ask again."

"Okay, okay. I'm getting up. Hold your fire. I'm unarmed," James repeated.

James carefully got up from his prone position when a high-intensity flashlight shone its beam into his face. He lifted his hands to cut down on the blinding light.

"Keep your hands where I can see them," came a different voice from somewhere behind the beam of light.

James' hands dropped abruptly to his sides.

"Who are you?"

"My name is James Hobbs and I…"

"Okay, James Hobbs, move towards the light."

James followed the order. He quickly found himself thrown face down onto the floor, a knee on his back holding him down.

"Any signs?" a voice asked.

"Nothing sir," another answered.

"Get up," the first voice ordered.

The beam of light pointed away from his face and he could see others in the room for the first time. A tall husky guy was holding a shotgun. Another tall man, but not as wide, stood right beside him and carried an automatic weapon over his shoulder. Two other men stood by the door and a fifth just outside it.

"What the hell are you doing here? You on a vacation or something?" The tall man with the shotgun asked with a grin.

There was some snickering from the doorway but the man with the automatic weapon showed no expression at all.

"I just arrived in town this afternoon and fell into this nightmare," James answered.

"Bullshit."

"I'm telling the truth."

"Bullshit. There is no way into this town or out for that matter. So don't lie to us."

"Listen, I live on a small island just off the coast. I lost contact with the mainland and ran out of supplies, so I came ashore and stumbled into this."

"An island, huh?"

"Right, just off the coast. I have a boat moored at the marina. I can prove it to you."

This caught their attention. They all looked at him and then at each other. No one said a word.

"Just might take you up on that," the guy with the shotgun finally said. "I'm Lieutenant Glenn. These are my men or at least what's left of them."

"What the hell happened here?" James asked.

"No time for that. Follow us and keep your mouth shut or we'll leave you for the Nesters."

"Nesters?"

"I told you to keep your mouth shut."

James and his newfound patrol exited the room and walked down the hall.

Everything was quiet.

What had happened to the gunfire? Where were the others? He had so many questions but knew better than to open his mouth. There was only one large flashlight for the 6 of them and the point man carried it. James found himself following along in the shadows. They continued down the hall kicking in doors but found nothing of interest. James wondered what exactly they were looking for. They arrived at the end of the hall and the point man signaled with his hand for them to stop.

They did.

The point man slowly opened the fire exit door and James thought he could hear the sound of something clicking against metal from somewhere down in the stairwell. It reminded him of a dog's nails clicking across a hardwood floor.

"Get back!" the point man screamed, as he lobbed something down the stairwell. All the men ran in the opposite direction. No one bothered to invite James, so he just followed along. They all sprinted back down the hallway when an explosion threw them to the ground. Shaken and scared James picked himself up, not bothering to wait for the help that probably wouldn't be offered anyway.

The others were already up and regrouping. One of the men picked up the fallen flashlight when an ungodly screech sounded from the stairwell.

"How many?" the Lieutenant asked.

"A lot," came the reply.

The sound of breaking glass from somewhere behind them grabbed their attention.

"We've been flanked."

"What..." James got out, just before a burst of automatic gunfire temporarily deafened him.

TALES FROM THE PARKLAND

James watched, panicked, as the men turned on smaller flash-lights attached to their shoulders. The hallway lit up and exposed the horrifying scene. From behind them, the spider things were crawling out of the vacant rooms. They were like ants swarming over the walls, ceiling, and floor. In front of them, the fire exit door gave way and even more of them poured out into the hallway.

All hell broke loose.

Every weapon in the little band's arsenal went off at once. Shotguns, automatic weapons, handguns. The spider things dropped like bugs sprayed with insecticide, but more continued to come.

"Get into a room," the Lieutenant ordered.

In a formation that looked like they'd practiced it a hundred times, the men, continuing to fire, backed into a room.

"Barricade the door."

The men threw whatever they could find against the door. James joined in and helped them move the bed across the room and dump it against the door.

The light from their shoulder flashlights threw eerie shadows across the walls.

"Everyone in the center of the room," the Lieutenant barked.

They all assembled in the center. Each man seemed to know exactly where he was supposed to be. They had their backs to one another so all sides were protected.

"Can you use a gun?" Lieutenant Glenn asked James.

"Uh, yes I think so," James answered.

"It's really easy. Point and pull the trigger."

"Should I bother to aim?" James asked, trying to be funny.

"Won't matter. The way I figure it, they'll hit us in a mass at-tack so if you pull the trigger, you're bound to hit something."

James felt sick. He didn't even know what these things were or what the hell was happening. His thoughts drifted again to his island as he stood waiting for whatever horror was next.

"They're at the window," one of the men announced.

"Okay, get ready. Remember to close the hole if someone goes down. Don't give them an opening," the Lieutenant ordered.

The barricade started to crumble as the things slammed them-selves against the door. James turned his head towards the window and saw at least eight of the things peering in at them. Then as if on cue they started to hammer away at the glass.

The barricade broke and the first wave swept towards them.

"Give them hell," the Lieutenant yelled.

Rounds of ammunition ripped the things to pieces, leaving them in scraps on the floor. The second wave charged in to the same effect.

Suddenly the window shattered and more of them attacked.

Automatic gunfire erupted beside James and without thinking or aiming he fired round after round into the creatures. The things dropped like stones but were soon replaced by more.

"How's your ammo?" the guy next to him yelled.

"Okay for now, you?"

"Plenty to spare, buddy. Plenty to spare."

A trio of shotgun blasts exploded, the awful screeching from the things almost drowning them out.

"Lob a grenade through the doorway," the Lieutenant yelled through the mayhem.

There was no answer but a few seconds later, from the hall-way, a thunderous roar erupted as the grenade detonated.

Then more sounds of live ammunition began.

"We must be near a nest. I've never seen so many of them attack at once."

"Keep firing. Leave your thoughts for a book."

The bed finally dropped to the floor and the entire doorway became exposed. The things flowed in like a tide, but the small group never slowed down and never quit, firing round after round into the obscene bodies of the things.

"Mike's down," someone screamed.

"Close the hole," the Lieutenant ordered.

"There's too many of them."

"Keep firing."

James looked around the room. They were surrounded. The whole thing seemed hopeless. He was running on pure instinct now. He watched the men try to drag Mike into their center. He spotted Mike's automatic weapon, instinctively picked it up and began firing.

"I want a couple more grenades through that doorway," the Lieutenant ordered over the din of gunfire.

"Shit." James heard from just behind him. He turned his head to see what had happened. A grenade that had missed its mark bounced off the inside wall and back towards them just as another wave of the things attacked.

The explosion ripped through the room and he saw at least a dozen of the things torn apart before his eyes. Suddenly something struck him on the side of the head and everything went black.

"That's it, you can do it." James could feel hands on him but couldn't make out who was speaking. "You're almost there, open your eyes. Come on, that's it."

James slowly opened his eyes. The sunlight filtering in from the window scorched his eyeballs. The pain in his head was terrible but it was the smell that made it worse.

James' eyes began to focus and he saw the Lieutenant kneeling beside him. Dried blood covered his face as well as his arms and everywhere else for that matter.

"Are you okay?" James asked.

"I've had better days," the Lieutenant answered. After deciding James was okay, he let himself sink to the floor.

"You sure you're okay?"

"I'll live," the Lieutenant replied.

"So, what happened? How the hell did we survive?"

"Firepower. Pure and simple."

James looked around and saw the others lying motionless on the floor.

"Are they all dead?" James asked, stunned.

The Lieutenant simply nodded.

"My God. What are we going to do?"

The Lieutenant lifted his head, which seemed like a chore, and stared at James for a moment before answering.

"We head for your island."

"Are you serious?"

"There's nothing left for us here. My squad is all dead, no reinforcements are coming, and those things just keep multiplying. So yes, I'm pretty serious."

James struggled to his feet and stood for a moment, slowly getting his equilibrium back. He stared at the bodies scattered on the floor. There were four human bodies and scores of things not quite human. James gagged back a few wretches. The taste in his mouth was awful. A warm breeze blew in through the broken window. He watched as the Lieutenant picked himself up and hobbled towards it.

"Try to scavenge as much weaponry and ammunition as you can. You never know when we may need it again," the Lieutenant said.

"You're serious about going to the island?" James asked.

"You have any better ideas?"

James searched the dead bodies for weapons and ammunition.

"We'll load up on as many supplies as we can carry along the way to the marina. I don't want to have to make another trip into the city for a while."

The two of them walked toward the marina after picking up supplies from abandoned stores along the way. "So, let me get this right," James said, as they walked along, recapping what he had just been told. "This has been going on for close to three weeks?"

"Yep. I was called into service from my base in South Carolina about one week into the incident."

"Incident, I think this might be more than an incident, don't you?" James asked.

"I guess I would," the Lieutenant said.

"And you have no idea what caused it?"

"Nope. There was lots of speculation but nothing concrete."

"Like what?"

"Well, I heard that some virus the Government was working on got loose. But we also had witnesses who said they saw something fall from the sky and crash into a forest not far from here, just before all hell broke loose."

"You're telling me this is some extraterrestrial event?"

"I'm not telling you anything but the stuff I've heard. Our Government never made a statement one way or the other. I guess there just wasn't enough time and then they stopped communicating."

"So just let me make sure I have this right. This so-called incident or event occurs and suddenly average everyday people start transforming into these spider things?"

"That's right," the Lieutenant answered, not bothering to look at James when he spoke.

The sun sat high overhead and the air around them was thick with moisture. The loads they carried weren't helping make the trip any more comfortable either.

They continued their walk towards the marina.

"These things or what do you call them, Nesters, spread across the continent in only a few weeks?" James asked.

"That's right."

"And when they sting you, you can transform into one of them within the day?"

"Yes, the turnover time is surprisingly quick."

James stopped walking for a minute and stared at the Lieutenant in disbelief. The Lieutenant didn't bother to stop and James watched him lug the gear down the street.

"Hey," James called out.

"What?"

"Wait up.

The Lieutenant didn't stop but did slow down to allow James to catch up.

"So, we have no communication with the outside world?"

"Correct. We lost contact about six days ago. Although I know there are still others alive, trapped within the nests."

"My God," James gasped.

"God has nothing to do with this," the Lieutenant offered.

They reached the waterfront with the sun beating down on them. Both were dead tired and soaking wet with perspiration. The grocery carts they pushed were filled with almost everything they'd need; canned goods, cereal, bottled water, beer, and loads of weapons and ammunition.

They crossed the main street and made their way to the marina to search for a bigger boat they could use. It wasn't long before they found a 20-foot yacht with the key still in the ignition.

After siphoning as much gas as they could from other boats, they searched for and eventually found a gas-powered generator. They struggled with it as they carried it to the yacht. Finally, they got it on board and prepared to leave.

James tried the ignition and the motor turned over smoothly. James turned to the Lieutenant with an enthusiastic smile. It quickly faded when he noticed movement on the beach. Thousands of the things were swarming over the soft sand. Thousands more it seemed were right behind them.

"Get this thing moving," the Lieutenant screamed, as he darted down the short ladder to the main deck. Sorting through the weapons they'd brought he finally found what he was looking for and carried it quickly to the other side of the yacht.

James tried the different levers and switches, hoping desperately to get a handle on how to work the yacht. He had hoped to have had more time to figure things out before having to pull out. He lifted his head to get his bearings when he noticed the beach again. The things were everywhere and closing on them fast. In desperation, he threw a lever and the boat started with a jolt and began to back up.

From the left side of the boat, an automatic weapon opened fire, startling James from his concentration. The yacht smacked into another boat moored behind them and James prayed he hadn't done any damage. He cranked the wheel and felt the yacht begin to turn. Scraping wood and metal reverberated throughout the boat.

The continuous automatic gunfire made it hard for James to concentrate. He continued cranking the steering wheel and as the yacht came around, he had a bird's-eye view of the marina. The things were climbing the fence and beginning to swarm down the pier.

James guessed they only had a minute or two before the things reached them. He decided there was no time to try to turn the yacht all the way around. He kept the yacht in reverse and with the automatic gunfire buying them some much needed time, he increased the engine's speed and crashed through any boats that were moored behind them.

"Get us out into the open water quick," the Lieutenant yelled.

"I'm trying," James shouted, as their yacht bounced off yet another boat.

The yacht continued its reversed course until it slammed into one of the docks, splintering it into pieces.

They were free.

James cranked the wheel and set them finally on a forward trajectory.

From what was left of the dock, several of the things managed to jump to the side of the yacht.

"Keep going. I'll go handle it," the Lieutenant said, as he hurried away.

They were in open water now and headed for the island. Would these things follow? Should he continue past his island until they'd put more distance between them? Was there anywhere in North America these things hadn't reached?

James heard a gunshot and then another. There was a horrible screeching and then quiet. He continued to pilot the yacht unaware of what was happening below.

"Lieutenant," James hollered, over the din of the engines. "Lieutenant," he screamed again, louder this time.

There was no answer. James wanted to go have a look but decided it was more important to put more distance between them and the mainland first.

It remained quiet and James became more worried. Was the Lieutenant dead? Were there still things onboard?

Suddenly, one of the creatures slammed itself against the Captain's window, trying desperately to get at James. James swerved the yacht to the left and then to the right, hoping to knock it off. The thing slid a bit but didn't fall off.

James began to panic.

"Duck," a voice called out.

Startled, James jumped to the side. The Lieutenant cocked the shotgun and pulled the trigger. Nothing happened. He did it again and still nothing. It was empty. Without thinking James grabbed the steering wheel and jerked it as far left as he could. The Lieutenant crashed into the far wall as James kept his eyes on the thing. The thing had almost flipped overboard but somehow managed to hold on.

Quickly, James spun the wheel to the far right. The yacht lurched awkwardly, skipping over its wake, which lifted it out of the water and slammed it back down again deep on its right side.

The thing lost its grip and flew through the air, splashing into the water below. James righted the yacht and steadied it as best he could, thanking God he hadn't capsized it.

The Lieutenant struggled to his feet and they both looked over the side. They spotted the thing thrashing in the water until finally it went under.

"You okay?" James asked.

"I'm fine. How are you doing?"

"I thought my heart stopped there for a second but I guess I'm okay."

"Well, it looks like our friends don't like the water very much," the Lieutenant said.

The two of them gazed back over the beachfront, now covered with the things.

"That just might be our salvation," James said. "If we can just keep water between them and us, we might be okay."

"Sooner or later we'll have to go back to the mainland for supplies you know."

"Let's worry about that later," James said, not wanting to even think about it.

The Lieutenant stretched out in one of the chairs. "Fine with me. Want a warm beer?"

BOGEYMAN

Chris Tucker generally ignored the panhandlers he passed each day on the way to the bus stop after leaving work. Today though, each one he passed caught his attention. Only half an hour earlier, Chris had received his walking papers and found himself suddenly unemployed from the hotel he'd worked at for over a decade. Was this what life had in store for him, he wondered as he eyed each panhandler he passed?

He couldn't imagine himself in their position but he wondered just what it took to fall so far off the radar. He'd received a fair compensation package so he'd be all right for the time being but the thought of having to rejoin the hostile world of the unemployed was daunting.

At home his wife, Mary and son, Ethan were oblivious to what had happened and Chris wondered how he'd be able to tell them.

"Spare some change," a dirty looking guy with no front teeth begged.

Chris looked down at the panhandler and made eye contact, something he usually never did. "Sorry," Chris said with a shrug. As he passed by, he thought he heard the panhandler growl. In the mood he was in he felt like turning and giving the guy an earful but decided what would be the point? The growl had unsettled him though. It sounded like something that would have come from an animal, not a human.

He dug his hands into his pant pockets to suppress the clanging of change. No use attracting the attention of other panhandlers.

It seemed to Chris that there was a panhandler on every street corner. Had it always been like this, he wondered? How could he have been so oblivious to them all?

A commotion up ahead snapped Chris from his thoughts. He lifted his gaze from the ground and looked towards the underpass. Sounds of an argument drifted towards him, not surprising considering the street trash who hung out under there. He normally crossed the street at this point to avoid any hassles and tonight would be no different, or so he thought.

He stood at the curb as cars raced by, waiting for a break in the traffic so he could cross the street.

The 102, the bus he took home, appeared on the horizon. Chris looked down at his watch and cursed. If he hadn't been stopped by that condescending Annie, who he knew would be sitting behind his desk tomorrow, he wouldn't be running late.

The bus pulled over and stopped a few blocks away to pick up or let off some passengers. Chris looked at the underpass again and then back across the road. He decided there was no way he'd be able to make it to the bus stop in time if he avoided the underpass.

Chris listened for a moment. Everything seemed calm by the underpass now. He turned to look for the bus and saw it easing back into traffic.

He had no choice.

The underpass was covered with graffiti and reeked of urine. Several crows pecked feverishly at what looked like a dead rat. Every second light was out, lending the area a surreal, shadowy quality. Chris kept his face down and his hands deep in his pockets clenched around the small amount of change he had.

"Hey buddy," a voice said, "spare some change?"

Chris kept walking.

A woman's voice whispered from the shadows. "My daughter's starving," she said, "anything will help."

A twinge of guilt sliced its way through Chris.

"Will work for food," another voice called out.

Chris felt the walls closing in on him. He picked up his pace, keeping his eyes on the ground before him.

He was almost through. Just ignore them he told himself.

"I know you," a menacing voice said from somewhere in the dark.

Chris almost stopped but managed to keep going.

"Hey, I know you," the voice said, more menacingly this time. "Come back here."

Chris walked faster.

"Still wet your bed?" the voice asked.

Chris stopped dead. He heard snickering from the shadows.

"So, you do remember."

Chris turned. He thought he recognized the voice, but it couldn't be who he thought. He took a few tentative steps forward. A panhandler limped from the shadows.

"What do you want?" Chris asked.

"For you to remember."

Chris studied him as he approached. He was overweight, shorter than Chris and wore a sneer that sent a shiver through Chris. He wasn't anyone he recognized but his voice was one he'd never forget. "I don't know what you're talking about," Chris finally managed.

"Yes you do, bed wetter."

"Why are you saying that?" Chris asked.

The panhandler grinned. "To help you remember."

"Remember what?"

"Me of course."

The panhandler limped closer. His face seemed to shift in the light but Chris decided it was only the shadows playing tricks.

"What do you want?" Chris asked again.

"The life you stole from me."

Chris frowned. "I don't even know you."

The panhandler limped even closer and with each step, his face altered, changed somehow. Somewhere deep within Chris's subconscious, a memory tried to surface but he couldn't quite put the pieces together.

"I have to go," Chris finally said. "You've mistaken me for someone else."

"But Chris," the panhandler said. "We have so much to catch up on."

Chris backed away, surprised the panhandler knew his name but found himself hesitant to leave.

"I can feel you remembering. My powers are beginning to awaken."

Chris shuffled his feet. He couldn't understand why he didn't just leave. There was something about this panhandler. Could it be possible they'd known each other once? Perhaps in high school?

"Can I have a quarter?"

Without a thought, Chris pulled a quarter from his pocket and held it out for the panhandler. The panhandler didn't take the quarter but instead clasped his hand over Chris's. Chris tried to pull away but it was as if his body was frozen in place.

A jolt ran through his body and a long-forgotten memory coursed through him. A time when he was just a young boy. A young boy who believed the Bogeyman lived under his bed.

Chris's head shot back and he dropped to the ground.

"Thank you," the panhandler said.

Chris felt numb. He couldn't move, no matter how hard he tried. A crowd of punks appeared from the shadows and circled him. Chris willed his body to get up but it wouldn't comply.

"Leave him," the panhandler said.

"Get out of the way, fatty," one of the punks said.

The largest of the punks stepped forward. "Yeah, before you get hurt."

There was a girl with them and she hustled over to Chris and rifled through his pockets. Chris could only watch helplessly.

The panhandler moved with incredible speed, the movement of his arms nothing more than a blur. The girl's head unceremoniously dropped from her body and rolled into the shadows of the underpass. Before any of the punks could react, the panhandler was on them, slicing and dicing until they were nothing more than slabs of bruised meat scattered around the underpass.

The panhandler looked down at Chris and smiled. "Welcome back old friend." He lifted Chris gently in his arms, bent his knees and pushed off like a loaded spring. They flew through the sky and disappeared into the inky blackness.

"Chris?" a woman's voice said. "Chris, wake up."

"Stop shaking me," Chris begged, holding his head.

Mary stood over him looking anxious. "Are you all right? Have you been drinking?"

"What happened?" he asked, still disoriented.

"You tell me. Ethan looked out the window when the bus went by and saw you lying on the lawn."

Chris dragged himself to his feet. "I don't know what happened but I had the strangest dream."

"Are you sure you're all right?" Mary asked.

Chris's head pounded as he rubbed his temples. "I think so."

"Well come inside, supper's almost ready." Mary took Chris's arm and helped him into the house.

Ethan sat in front of the television playing a video game but looked up when his father walked into the room. "Why were you lying on the lawn?"

"I was looking for grubs."

Ethan thought about this for a second and finding that to be a suitable answer went back to playing his game.

"I'm going upstairs to change and wash up," Chris announced to anyone listening. He walked up the narrow stairs and straightened a picture that seemed crooked to him.

In the washroom, he threw water on his face and grabbed a towel to dry off. Afterward, he hung it back up and left the washroom. As he entered his bedroom, he noticed a rather large ass sticking out from under his bed. Startled, he stood frozen in place. "Hey," he called out but there was no answer. He approached the ass and gave it a slight kick. "Hey." There was still no answer. "Mary," he shouted.

Mary ran into the room a few seconds later. "What is it?"

"Look," Chris said, pointing at the large ass still sticking out from under their bed.

"What am I looking at?" she asked.

"That," he said again, still pointing at the ass.

"The rug?"

Chris marched closer to the ass and pointed at it again. "No, this."

"Are you sure you're okay?"

"You're telling me you can't see this enormous rump sticking out from under our bed?"

Mary frowned. "I don't have time for this." Mary turned and left the room.

Chris stared at the butt as he listened to Mary's fading footsteps.

"Pull me out," the butt said. Well, not the butt but whoever was attached to it.

"I'm going to call the police."

"Won't do any good. They won't be able to see me any more than your wife did."

Chris gave the butt a kick.

"Stop doing that and pull me out."

"Who are you?" Chris asked.

"Let's just say I owe you a quarter."

Chris looked at the struggling rump and recognized the pants. It was the panhandler from the underpass. Chris grabbed his ankles and pulled him from under the bed. The panhandler rolled onto his back and heaved great breaths of air into his lungs.

"Thanks," he said.

"What are you doing here?" Chris asked.

"I brought you home."

Chris laughed. "How, in your bum mobile?"

"That's funny."

Chris paced the room. He straightened different pictures and put a few things away as he did so. "I'm going mad."

"Not entirely," the panhandler said.

Chris stopped. He turned to the panhandler and stared at him. "Enough games. Who are you?"

"The Bogeyman," the panhandler answered.

"Get real."

The panhandler stood up and dusted himself off. "You should vacuum under the bed every decade or so you know."

"I want to know who you are and what you were doing under my bed."

The panhandler's face seemed to alter again. "I just told you, are you deaf?"

"Yes, the Bogeyman. I got that but I want to hear the truth. Is Mary in on this?"

The beggar moved from the side of the bed and held his hands out. "Have a seat," he said.

"Don't tell me what to do in my own home," Chris said.

"Suit yourself," the panhandler said. He moved to the bed and sat down. "Listen closely. Believe me or not, I am the Bogeyman. Actually, I'm the Bogeyman under the bed. Not to be confused with the Bogeyman in the closet or down in the basement or up in the attic or in the hallway…"

"Stop, I don't want to hear anymore."

The panhandler patted the bed, gesturing for Chris to calm down and sit beside him. Chris refused.

"I know you believe me," the panhandler said.

"No, I don't."

The panhandler grinned. "Yes, you do. Otherwise, I wouldn't be gaining my power back. You see, we bogeymen can only exist if you believe in us."

"What are you talking about?" Chris asked, clearly becoming frustrated. He felt his head pounding worse than ever.

"Think back, way back," the panhandler said. "When you were just a little boy, you imagined me and I became real. I was the Bogeyman under your bed. I'd make noises in the middle of the night and brush against your ankles when you climbed into bed. I whispered naughty thoughts into your mind while you slept." The panhandler paused. "Remember?"

Chris moved closer to the panhandler. He studied him hoping for some flash of remembrance. "Why are you back then? Where did you go?"

"Good questions," the panhandler said. "I became homeless, forgotten, devoid of purpose."

"Don't be melodramatic."

"It's true," the panhandler said. "As you got older you forgot about me. You no longer believed and basically, I became an unemployed Bogeyman."

"Why didn't you just move on to another boy or girl?"

"It doesn't work that way," the panhandler said.

"How does it work?" Chris asked.

"I was led to believe that I would fade away and be reincarnated into another Bogeyman but I have since found out that's not what happens at all."

Chris finally sat down on the bed beside his Boogeyman. "So, what does happen?"

"We're forgotten and find ourselves roaming with no purpose. Many of us go mad. We become what society fears. We are the killers who are never caught, the beggars on the street, the crazy people who speak to themselves and make you uncomfortable. Ghosts that haunt houses…"

"Why are you back?" Chris interrupted.

"I don't know," the Bogeyman answered. "Fate, destiny, you name it, but many things had to come together to make this work. You would have had to become susceptible in some way. Has there been a recent upheaval in your life?"

Chris got off the bed and straightened the drapes. "I lost my job today."

"Maybe that's it. You felt scared and helpless and by sheer co-incidence, it led you to me."

Chris felt exhausted. "So what now?"

The Bogeyman stood up and walked to Chris and put a loving arm around him. "Guess I'm moving in."

"No, no, no." Chris grasped his head as if it was about to explode.

"It'll be all right."

"No, it won't," Chris said. "I don't want you haunting my house or doing whatever it is you do."

"Come on, buddy, I wouldn't do that to you. That's kid's stuff. I just need a place to crash and someone to believe in me. I won't make a peep and I'll make one hell of a security system. Anyone breaks into your place and I'll rip them to pieces and paint the walls with their blood."

"Don't know if my wife would appreciate that," Chris said.

The Bogeyman gave Chris a tight hug. "Okay, no wall painting."

"I don't know."

"Let's cut to the chase," the Bogeyman said. "I can't leave anyway, I'm your creation and until you forget about me again, I'm here to stay. Why don't we try to make it advantageous for both of us?"

"You can't even fit under the bed anymore."

"That is a problem."

"So?"

"I'll get back in shape."

"Maybe you could live down in the basement?" Chris suggested.

"No."

"Why not?" Chris asked.

"Because I'm not a basement Bogeyman, I'm an under the bed Bogeyman."

"That's ridiculous."

"No, those are the rules."

"Dad," Ethan's call interrupted their conversation.

Both Chris and the Bogeyman turned as Ethan entered the room.

"What are you doing?" Ethan asked.

Before Chris could answer the Bogeyman's eyes lit up and a grin appeared across his face. Without warning, he advanced on Ethan.

"Stop," Chris shouted.

Ethan jumped, startled by his father's command. Even the Bogeyman stopped in his tracks.

"Don't touch him," Chris demanded.

"But he's so fresh. I'd be able to regain all my powers in no time with that tasty morsel."

Wide-eyed, Ethan asked, "Don't touch who?"

Chris moved towards them. "I'm sorry, it's okay."

The Bogeyman smiled. "Really?"

"Not you. Stay away from him."

"Make up your mind," the Bogeyman said.

"What?" Ethan asked.

"Nothing." Chris patted Ethan on the head. "Go downstairs and I'll be down in a minute."

Ethan eyed him with concern but without another word, he disappeared from the room and went back downstairs.

Chris turned to the Bogeyman. "What the hell do you think you're doing?"

"Nothing."

"You were about to attack my son."

"I was going to do no such thing."

"Yes, you were."

"No, I was not."

Chris grabbed the Bogeyman but let go when a sinister-sounding snarl emanated from him. "Get the hell out of my home," Chris ordered.

The snarls stopped. "And where am I supposed to go?" the Bogeyman asked.

"I don't care," Chris told him.

"Have you no compassion?" the Bogeyman asked. "I'm homeless with nowhere to go. Plus, I'm unemployed because of you."

"Cry me a river," Chris said. "I just lost my job so don't tell me how bad you've got it."

"I'm sorry, I forgot."

"It's not your problem but you are mine."

"So what are we going to do?" the Bogeyman asked.

"Well, you can't stay here."

"Why not?"

Chris plopped back down on the bed. "Because I'd always be worried for the safety of my wife and son."

"You can trust me."

"Can I?"

The Bogeyman sat down beside him. "No," he admitted.

Chris looked at the Bogeyman. "So you would attack them?"

"Most likely."

"But why? I offered you our basement."

"I don't know. It's in my nature, I guess. Hell, you made me. You tell me why I do the things I do."

Chris flopped down on the bed and stared at the ceiling. As he lay there he thought back on his childhood and it came back to him. "Carl Brown."

"What?" the Bogeyman asked.

"Carl Brown. I made you up because I wanted to punish Carl for picking on me."

"Is he the guy I pushed off the slide and who broke both his arms?"

Chris grinned as he thought back on the incident. "Yep, that's him."

The Bogeyman stretched out on the bed and placed his hands behind his head. "Those were the days."

Chris sprang from the bed and paced the room like a caged tiger. "I think I have an idea," he announced.

"Oh yeah?"

"You mentioned there are others like you, the…" Chris paused to think.

"The forgotten ones?"

"Yeah, that's it. Are there many of them?"

"Sure, but I only know about a dozen or so on a first name basis."

"Could you all live together in one place?"

"I guess, as long as we each had our own space."

Chris became excited as he formulated his plan. "How can we locate them?"

"Are you planning to move them all in here?" The Bogeyman shook his head. "I wouldn't advise it. There's a lot of rivalry among us and things could turn nasty for your family."

"Don't worry about it, I have it covered. Just find me more bogeymen."

"Okay, but don't say I didn't warn you."

The two left the house, sneaking out the back door so there would be no excuses to make to Mary. Chris was more scared of Mary's wrath than any bogeyman's. The Bogeyman picked Chris up and with a bend of his knees, the two of them sprang into the night sky.

"Jupiter," Chris repeated the name. "Okay, that makes unlucky thirteen. Are there any more of you around?" Chris searched the faces of the bogeymen who now stood around him in the underpass.

The thirteen bogeymen all shook their heads.

"Perfect, so now I know you all and I believe in you, so you must be regaining some of your powers."

A few of the bogeymen smiled and clenched their fists as others let out roars that rolled like thunder.

"One big, happy family," Chris announced. "Can any of you read my thoughts yet?"

Just over half of the bogeymen nodded.

"Good. I'm sure the rest of you will catch up soon enough." A smile spread across his face with this new accomplishment. "We're all set then. Let's find you a home."

A mighty, horrific roar ripped through the crowd of bogeymen as they fell in step behind Chris and left the underpass.

The doors to the Parliament Hotel opened electronically as Chris stepped in front of them. "Remember what I told you," Chris reminded them.

They grunted back at him.

"And you're sure they won't be able to see you?" Chris asked.

"Yes, we've regained our full powers and can appear and disappear at will," his childhood Bogeyman said.

"Then why can I still see you?"

"Because you're the believer."

Chris entered the front lobby and a twinge of uncertainty flooded through him. All the years he'd put into the place only to be discarded without a thought. They'll remember me now, he told himself.

"Hi Mr. Tucker," a bellman greeted him.

"Hi Stewart," he answered back. "Is Mr. St. Laurent in?"

"I think he's in his office but he left instructions not to be disturbed."

Chris turned towards a door that led to the executive offices. He nodded his head towards it and one of the bogeymen moved to the door.

Chris turned back to the bellman. "That's okay, he'll see me."

The bellman looked nervous. "Maybe I should call up first."

"Sure."

Before the bellman could make his call, the phones were ripped from the front desk by some of the bogeymen.

"What the hell's happening?" the bellman asked, ducking his head as phones flew across the lobby. Beside him, the door leading to the executive offices exploded off its hinges as one of the bogeymen crashed through it.

The other bogeymen began to stomp their feet until the ground beneath them shook.

Chris staggered to the bellman. "It must be an earthquake. Pull the fire alarm and help evacuate the guests."

The bellman ran off and Chris soon heard the sound of the fire alarms going off. He smiled and walked through the gaping hole that led to the executive offices.

The bogeymen followed.

As Chris marched up the stairs, a half-dressed André St. Laurent and Annie Blot appeared at the top of them.

"What are you doing here?" St. Laurent demanded.

"Just coming to pay a visit."

"You were told not to enter the hotel premises again."

"So, fire me." Chris looked past St. Laurent at Annie. "A little job interview, Annie?"

Annie straightened her blouse. "It's a dog-eat-dog world, Chris."

"Remember that," Chris said and signaled the bogeymen to begin.

St. Laurent stormed down the stairs. "Out of my way you idiot."

Chris stood aside and as St. Laurent approached him one of the bogeymen launched him like a rocket back up the stairs. Annie stared in disbelief as his body smashed into the wall and dropped to the floor.

Chris casually continued up the stairs. "I have a family to support," he told her. "I'm not an employee number. Did you give that any thought?"

Although Annie seemed frightened, she made a brave attempt at concealing it. "It's just business…"

Chris interrupted her. "I guess you'll understand then what I have to do to protect my assets." He waved the rest of the bogeymen on and they raced past him, dragging Annie and St. Laurent back into the offices above.

The screams were awful. Chris decided not to bother going up until it was over. He nervously looked down the stairs but the alarms were loud enough to prevent anyone from hearing the carnage happening behind him.

Eventually, his Bogeyman appeared. "It's done," he said.

"Did it work like you promised?" Chris asked.

"Yes."

"What about his computer?"

"You're in."

Chris grabbed the railing and propelled himself up the stairs. He stopped at the top, nervous of what he might find but the place was exactly as he'd left it earlier today. No blood, no body parts, no damage.

The bogeymen were lined up along the walls leading to the GM's office which now stood open. Chris tentatively approached it.

Inside the office, more of the bogeymen played darts. The dartboard was the living face of St. Laurent which was nicely mounted on the wall. As each dart penetrated his face St. Laurent screamed.

Chris looked at it in wonder. "How did you manage that?"

"Once you gave us this hotel as a home it became a living entity. A part of us, so to speak. Anything can happen at the Parliament now." The Bogeyman stepped back and pointed an arm out. Chris followed the gesture and noticed Annie, now molded into the shape of a chair sitting behind the computer. "Have a seat," the Bogeyman suggested.

Chris noticed Annie's eyes moving as he approached. "As you said, it's a dog eat dog world. Now, kiss my ass." Chris unceremoniously had a seat. He looked up at the Bogeyman. "You'll make sure they are unnoticeable to anyone else right?"

"As you wish but I don't see why."

Chris looked through St. Laurent's computer files and found what he was looking for. He let out a sigh of relief. His dismissal announcement hadn't been posted yet and was dated for the next day. He made a few changes to the letter which would explain St. Laurent and Annie's love for each other and why they'd decided to run away together. It would also mention how after meeting with Chris Tucker, he'd decided to offer the GM position to him.

Of course, there would be meetings with the board members but with the help of the bogeymen, Chris didn't see a problem with his self-appointed promotion.

Chris turned off the computer, satisfied, but now he worried how mad Mary was going to be at him for missing dinner. He let a fart rip as he got up from his chair. "Sorry Annie, my bad." He grabbed a handful of darts from the desk and decided dinner was probably already cold.

BIG BOY

Peter hated it at daycare. At nine years old he felt he should be able to stay at home alone. Usually he was in school but today was a PD day. What made it worse was the fact that his mother didn't work so he couldn't understand why he wasn't home with her.

"What are you doing?"

Peter put down the pencil he'd been sketching with. He turned to see who was speaking and saw Maggie standing behind him. He flipped over the paper so she couldn't see what he'd been sketching.

"Nothing."

"Doesn't look like nothing."

"What do you want Maggie?"

Maggie's expression changed as her lower lip started to tremble. Peter suddenly felt guilty. He knew she liked him and for a six-year-old, she wasn't as bad as some of the others at daycare but he hated being bothered while he sketched.

"I'm sorry Maggie," he said. "I was just sketching."

Maggie looked at him as if unsure what to do. "I didn't mean to bug you."

Peter slid his chair around to face her. "You're not bugging me."

"Then what's the matter?"

"I don't want to be here."

"How come?" she asked.

Peter looked at Maggie with her brown curly hair and her dark brown eyes and said, "I don't know, I just don't."

"Can I see your picture?"

"It's not done yet."

"That's okay."

Peter decided to change the subject. "Do you like it here?"

"Yes," she answered. "How come you don't?"

"I'm too old for daycare. Besides, my mom's home so I'd rather be there playing video games."

Maggie looked at him as if trying to think of what to say.

"Wouldn't you rather be home?" he asked.

"There's no kids to play with there," she told him. "How come you never play with us?"

"Because there's no one here my age."

Maggie turned away and looked into the other room. After a moment she pointed to a boy playing with some toy soldiers. "Sean's seven, why don't you play with him?" she asked.

Peter followed her pointed finger and frowned. "He's a loser. All he does is drool over those stupid toy soldiers all day."

"I thought boys like playing with soldiers?"

"That's for kids," he told her.

"You're only nine, Peter Weston," she said. "You're a kid just like us." Maggie didn't wait for a response but instead turned and walked into the next room to be with the other kids.

Peter watched her go. He didn't feel like sketching anymore. He put the pencil back into the jar where they kept all the other pencils and crayons and stood up. He folded his half-finished picture and put it in his pants pocket and walked to the window.

Outside, it was the perfect day. Not too hot and not too cold. The sky was as blue as the Arabian Sea he'd read about in his adventure books. He wished he could have an adventure.

Peter read a lot. He tended to do that when his parents fought. It seemed to Peter that was all they did. He noticed lately that his dad was coming home later and later and that as soon as he walked in the door they were fighting.

Peter hated the yelling.

He swore that when he was a parent, he'd never yell in front of his kids. He remembered how embarrassed he was when Aunt Sara had to come over in her squad car. Aunt Sara was his dad's older sister and a policewoman. He never understood what they were fighting about but he knew his mom hated that his dad traveled so much.

As he stared out the window, he remembered the fight his parents had last night. His dad had told his mom to get off the couch and get a job. Needless to say, that hadn't gone over well. Peter had thought of running away but instead, he'd picked up a book and disappeared into it.

A flock of birds burst into the air, breaking Peter's train of thought. His thoughts turned to school as the birds disappeared into the distance. If he was at school right now, he thought, he'd be at recess with his friends.

A loud boom went off in the distance.

Peter turned to see if anyone else had heard it but no one had seemed to.

"Stop jumping around," Mrs. Carmichael shouted from the kitchen.

So someone else had heard it, Peter thought.

He turned back to the window to check if he could see anything. He saw nothing but the beautiful day he was missing out on by being stuck inside.

A second louder boom echoed in Peter's ears.

"What are you kids doing…" Mrs. Carmichael's voice was cut off by a third even louder boom. This time the whole house shook and the floor seemed to heave up from underneath Peter.

Peter crashed to the floor.

The house stopped shaking but Peter continued to lay on the floor. The sound of some of the younger kids crying brought Mrs. Carmichael into the living room.

"Everyone okay?" she asked, picking up one of the crying toddlers. "I think we may have had an earthquake but it's over now."

Peter got up off the floor. "I don't think it was an earthquake," he said.

"Of course it was," Mrs. Carmichael responded, "but we're all okay."

"No," Peter continued, "I heard an explosion outside."

Mrs. Carmichael rocked the toddler in her arms. She walked towards Peter, glancing out the window.

"Can you see anything?" Peter asked.

As she looked out the window she said, "I can see smoke off in the distance."

Peter walked to the window. "Think it's terrorists?"

"I doubt it," she said. "Maybe we should turn on the TV and see if the news channel has anything on it."

The phone in the kitchen rang and she turned to Peter. "Can you hold him for a minute?" Without waiting for an answer, she handed the little boy to Peter and hurried off to the kitchen.

Peter looked at the child as if it was a fish he'd just pulled out of the water. The little boy looked up at Peter and smiled. Peter turned and gazed out the window. Billowing smoke rose in the air, off in the distance. An awful lot of smoke, he thought.

"Are you sure?" Peter heard Mrs. Carmichael ask from the kitchen. He stepped away from the window and moved closer to the doorway to the kitchen so he could listen in.

"You're on your way?"

Peter felt frustrated that he could only hear one side of the conversation.

"Is it safe for us to stay here?" She paused. "You're sure? Okay, how long?"

Peter heard her walk towards him so he stepped back to the window. Mrs. Carmichael poked her head through the doorway and then disappeared again.

"All right, we'll be here," she told whoever was on the phone with her.

Peter heard her hang up the phone. The TV in the kitchen came on. He tried to listen but she'd turned the volume down.

The phone rang again.

"Hello," Mrs. Carmichael answered, "Yes, I heard. I don't know. Okay, see you soon."

Mrs. Carmichael walked into the room. "Brandy, Josh, your parents are on the way to pick you up so get your stuff ready please."

"Is everything okay?" Peter asked.

"Everything's fine," she assured him.

"What's the news saying?"

She reached out and grabbed the boy from Peter's arms. "Nothing for you to worry about."

She turned and walked back into the kitchen. Peter followed her to the door but she stopped in front of him, blocking the entrance. "Go play," she told him, "I have to make a few calls. As she started to slide the door shut, the phone rang again.

Peter stood there as she shut the door in his face. He turned away and walked through the living room, toys littered across the floor, and made his way to the family room. He passed the other children, who it seemed had forgotten what had just happened and were once again happily playing.

Maybe Mom will call, Peter thought as he entered the family room. He waited for a few moments to make sure Mrs. Carmichael was still busy before turning on the TV. He flipped through the channels, always keeping an ear out for anyone who might come into the room.

Peter finally came across a channel that had a video of the smoke he'd seen, rising in the air. He looked at the TV screen in wonder as flames shot out from within the smoke. Must be a doozy, he thought as he stood mesmerized in front of the TV.

A young woman appeared on the screen with the smoke as her backdrop. She held a microphone and seemed about to speak but instead looked back at the fire as if it might be sneaking up on her. Peter thought to himself what a cool job that must be. He thought that maybe it might be something he'd like to do when he got older. He looked over his shoulder to see if any of the kids had decided to follow him in but the coast was clear.

"From where I'm standing, I can easily feel the heat of the fire," a woman's voice said.

Peter quickly turned to face the TV.

"We're standing not far from what used to be the LKJ Technology Headquarters," the announcer stated.

Peter knew the building. They used to pass it when they went to that Tex-Mex restaurant nearby for dinner. He remembered it because it had a big fighter jet out front that looked as if it was about to take off. Peter continued to stare at the TV.

"At this time, we have no idea what caused the three explosions that rocked this neighborhood just a short time ago."

Peter heard the phone ring again. Good, he thought, that should keep Mrs. Carmichael busy.

"Here come some firefighters from the building," the announcer said. "Jim, can you get them into the shot?"

The camera moved to the right and half a dozen firefighters came into view.

Maybe I could be a firefighter, Peter thought to himself.

Peter watched as the firefighters got closer. From off to the side, several other firefighters and some police officers came into view. As the two groups met, the first group of firefighters suddenly attacked the others without warning. Were those axes they were carrying, Peter wondered. He watched in horror as blood flowed copiously from the downed bodies. The crazy firefighters continued hacking the downed bodies into pieces with their axes.

"Are you getting this?" the announcer screamed.

From behind the crazy firefighters appeared dozens of others who quickly charged into the melee. It looked to Peter as if they had weapons as well. He wondered if his aunt Sara was there and started to feel sick to his stomach.

"Get to the van," the reporter shrieked. The picture from the camera became jerky and Peter could tell they were running. The sound of screams seemed to be right behind them. Suddenly the picture pitched at a strange angle and crashed to the ground. The picture went dead.

Peter stood there in a daze. What had just happened?

"Peter," a voice yelled.

Peter jumped.

"Peter, where are you?"

He quickly realized it was Mrs. Carmichael calling him. He turned the TV off in a hurry and grabbed a book from the shelf to make it seem like he'd just been browsing through them. His hands shook as he held it.

"Peter, your father is on the phone."

A feeling of relief flooded through him. He threw the book onto the shelf and ran to the phone.

"Hello," he said after he took the phone from Mrs. Carmichael's beefy hand.

"Hi buddy, how you doing?" his father asked.

"Good."

"I'm going to come and pick you up, okay?"

"Sure," Peter answered. After a pause, he asked, "How come Mom isn't going to pick me up?"

"I can't get a hold of her but I'm leaving work right now."

Peter thought about what he'd seen on the TV and wanted to mention it to his dad but he was afraid that maybe his dad wouldn't come and get him if he found out what was going on.

"How long until you get here?"

"Should be there in about thirty minutes," he told Peter. "Can you put Mrs. Carmichael back on?"

"Okay, see you soon." He didn't want to hand the phone to Mrs. Carmichael. As a matter of fact, he didn't want to get off the phone at all. He wanted to keep talking to his dad until he rang Mrs. Carmichael's doorbell. As he was about to hand the phone to

Mrs. Carmichael, he heard his father saying something. Peter put the phone back to his ear. "Dad?"

"Stay put and wait for me, okay?"

"Okay."

"I don't want to have to come looking for you so stick around and be ready, okay?"

Peter didn't like the sound of his dad's voice. He almost sounded scared. "Okay," Peter said again. He handed the phone to Mrs. Carmichael.

Across the kitchen, he noticed the small TV on the counter was still on. As he watched it, he recognized the strip mall which was only a short distance away from the daycare. He wondered why they'd be showing that. It was such a dinky mall, he thought. Nothing exciting ever happened there.

Today was different though.

On the TV screen, people were running everywhere. No, they weren't just running, they were being chased. Peter watched in horror, as a woman holding a child was tackled to the ground and attacked by the crazy people.

Peter gasped.

Mrs. Carmichael heard the gasp and looked at Peter and then at the TV. With a few hurried steps, she walked to the TV and shut it off. "Go in the other room, please."

Peter stood staring at the black screen.

"Peter."

Peter looked up at Mrs. Carmichael.

"Go and do something."

Peter walked out of the room, his mind racing. Maybe he should try to call his mom, he thought. No, his dad said she wasn't home. Then it occurred to him, what if she'd gone to the mall to pick up something? He started to feel scared. He wasn't going to cry, he convinced himself. He was a big boy now.

Peter wandered into the living room and for the first time in a while, he liked being with the other kids. He sat down on the couch and watched them play. Everything was going to be all right he tried to assure himself.

The doorbell rang and Peter jumped.

Mrs. Carmichael hurried down the hallway, passed the living room and answered the door. A woman walked in and Peter felt let down when it wasn't his mom. One of the younger boys got up and ran to his mother and gave her a big hug.

Peter heard a car pull into the laneway and raced to the window. A frown appeared on his face as another one of the mothers got out of the car and hustled to the house.

Peter looked at the clock on the mantle and saw that half an hour had gone by since he'd spoken with his father. Where was he, he worried?

He looked around the room. Mrs. Carmichael was on the phone again. Maggie sat on the couch beside him reading a comic book. Sean continued to play with the toy soldiers and two of the other kids were playing a board game.

Peter got up and walked to the window. His father still wasn't there.

Cars had been racing up and down the street for the last little while and Peter thought he'd even heard a crash and screams. Mrs. Carmichael had convinced him he'd only been imagining it.

"Grab your things, we have to go," Mrs. Carmichael suddenly called out.

Peter turned away from the window. "Go where?" he asked.

"No time to explain," she said. "Grab your knapsack and let's go."

Peter turned back to the window.

"Peter, now!" Mrs. Carmichael ordered.

A sense of confusion washed through Peter. He didn't want to leave before his dad got there. "But my dad's coming," he said.

"There's been an accident and if he's not here yet he's probably stuck somewhere."

"I'm going to wait," Peter announced.

"No, you're not. Now grab your things, we're going."

Mrs. Carmichael helped the two younger kids with their knapsacks. "Sean put down the soldiers. I'm not going to tell you again."

Peter peeked out the window but there was still no sign of his dad.

Something, which sounded like a scream, followed by a low and long moan caught everyone's attention.

"What was that?" asked Maggie.

"Forget your things," Mrs. Carmichael said. "We have to leave, now." Mrs. Carmichael fumbled through her purse and pulled out a set of keys. "Come on," she said.

Peter didn't know what to do. His dad had told him to sit tight and wait for him but Mrs. Carmichael was making them leave.

Peter danced on the spot like a toy that had bumped against a wall but kept trying to go forward anyway. He grew more frustrated as the seconds ticked by.

"Come on Peter," Maggie said.

"One sec, I have to grab my Epi," Peter answered.

"Hurry up then," Mrs. Carmichael said.

Peter thought he heard fear in her voice.

Peter ran down the hall for his Epi. He hadn't had an allergic reaction to peanuts in a while but he never went anywhere without it. He grabbed his Epi off the kitchen table and stopped for a moment to look out through the sliding doors which led to the backyard. He looked back down the hallway at Mrs. Carmichael and the other kids and then back at the sliding doors. His father's voice echoed in his mind, telling him to sit tight until he got there.

"Come on," Mrs. Carmichael yelled.

Peter ran for the sliding doors.

"Peter!"

Peter ignored Mrs. Carmichael's call and instead unlocked the sliding door and slipped through into the backyard.

The backyard was fenced in on three sides by tall cedar hedges. Peter looked around, feeling trapped, trying to decide what to do. He peeked around the corner of the house but couldn't see anyone. He pressed himself against the side of the house and inched quietly towards the front yard. As he approached the front of the house, he heard everyone leaving the house.

Peter got down on his belly and crawled toward the wrap-around porch. There was space enough for him to squeeze under so he dragged himself along the grass and under the porch.

He could watch for his dad from under here, he thought, or go back into the house after they'd left.

Peter looked at the laneway and spotted Mrs. Carmichael bent over the back seat of her car. Probably buckling the kids into their seats.

Peter heard a low moan from down the street.

Mrs. Carmichael popped out of the car and looked down the street. Peter tried to see what she was looking at but couldn't make anything out. He saw the expression on Mrs. Carmichael's face though and it made him shiver.

Peter watched as she slammed the car door shut and raced around to the driver's side. As she climbed in, she let out a horrible scream. Half a dozen people converged on the car, dragging Mrs.

Carmichael out of it. Peter heard the kids screaming from inside the car as some of the crazy people climbed in.

The car shook as if possessed.

The sound of the screaming kids filled the air. Peter held his hands to his ears.

Down the street, a high-pitched wail cut through the screams. The car stopped shaking and a low moan drifted from the car.

Peter pushed himself deeper under the porch but was careful not to lose sight of the crazy people. He watched as they stood around the car moaning. Then, without warning, they ran down the street towards where the wail had come from.

Once Peter felt it was safe, he dragged himself through the dirt and climbed out from underneath the porch. Cautiously, he walked toward the car. He saw Mrs. Carmichael's plump legs first, sticking out from behind the front wheel. When he came around the side of the car he gasped. Her blouse had been ripped off exposing her sagging left breast which was covered in blood. Peter looked away but not before he saw her face which looked like it was missing its nose.

He walked closer, trying not to look. "Mrs. Carmichael?"

He got no response.

"Mrs. Carmichael," he said again.

Peter peeked into the car and saw blood splattered all over the seats. He quickly turned away and wondered if he should hide under the porch again until his dad came, or should he try to make it home? Mom might be back, he hoped.

As he turned away, a groan from the car startled him.

Another groan.

Peter stared at the car, frozen.

"Hello?" he called out.

The groan turned to crying.

He recognized the crying.

Peter took a look around and when he decided there were no crazy people close by, he ran to the side of the car and looked in.

Maggie crawled out from under the bodies of Sean and one of the other girls from the daycare. Peter rushed to her and helped pull her from the car. She was covered in splattered blood.

"Are you okay?" Peter asked.

Maggie grabbed onto him, her body trembling from her sobs.

"It's okay," he told her, "I'll protect you." He had no idea how he would do such a thing but it sounded like the right thing to say.

Maggie squeezed tighter.

"We have to go back into the house so I can call my mom," he told her.

She loosened her hold.

Peter eased her away and wiped away the tears that streamed down her face. "Come on."

Maggie followed Peter to the house but as they climbed onto the porch, they heard something smash from inside.

"What was that?" Maggie whispered.

Before Peter could answer, a face appeared in the bay window and looked out at them. Blood smeared all over his face.

Maggie screamed and the face disappeared.

"Run," Peter said, grabbing Maggie's hand as he pulled her away from the house.

They ran four houses down before Peter said, "Let's get under one of the porches and hide."

Maggie nodded and followed him across the front lawn. Peter helped her squeeze under the porch and followed quickly after her.

"I want my mommy," Maggie said with tears in her eyes.

"Me too."

He didn't particularly like touching girls or even have them touch him for that matter but he put his arm around Maggie anyway because that's what big boys did.

A small group of people ran by the front of the house but Peter and Maggie weren't sure if they were the crazy people or not so they stayed hidden.

"When can we leave?" Maggie asked.

"I don't know," Peter replied.

"Are we going to be okay?"

"I think so," Peter said. "I don't think they can see us under here.

Maggie inched closer to Peter. They watched as more people ran by. A question itched in Peter's mind. What if those people running by were normal and they were all leaving? What if they were left behind with the crazy people?

"We have to go," Peter said.

"You sure?"

Peter turned on his side and looked at Maggie who was still covered in blood. "We have to get to my house, it's close by. My dad said he was on his way and when he doesn't find me at day-care he'll go check at home."

Maggie started to cry again.

"It'll be okay," Peter assured her. "I'll protect you."

Maggie gave him a hug.

"We have to get going though before he comes and doesn't find me and drives away."

Maggie nodded and let go.

When everything seemed clear, the two of them climbed out from under the porch.

"Which way?" Maggie asked.

Peter pointed down the street to their left. Everything was quiet. No sound of cars or people. The two of them kept close to the houses as they walked along, trying not to expose themselves to anyone who might be watching. Maggie reached over and grabbed Peter's hand. Peter smiled at her.

The two of them walked in silence.

As they approached the Miller's house, Peter spotted Bobby Miller laying in the front yard. Peter abruptly stopped.

"What's the matter?" Maggie asked.

"There's a body."

Maggie looked at where Peter pointed and gasped. "Is he alive?"

"I don't know."

"Should we check and see?" Maggie asked.

"I don't think we should," he answered.

The two of them stuck close to the houses as they approached Bobby Miller's body. Peter could see the blood on Bobby and could hear the flies already buzzing around him. Peter tightened his grip on Maggie and pulled her away. "We got to keep going," he told her.

Neither looked back.

As they got closer to Peter's house, they found more and more bodies, or at least what was left of them, laying in pools of blood. Peter told Maggie not to look and although she tried her best, she still stole a glance or two.

"What happened?" Maggie asked.

"I don't know Maggie but we'll be okay," he told her. "We just have to stick together."

Peter and Maggie approached Peter's house. Peter noticed his mother's car in the laneway. Why hadn't she picked me up, he wondered? They walked up to the car but Peter was afraid to look inside. He finally screwed up the courage and peered through the side window.

The car was empty.

"Is this your dad's car?" Maggie asked.

"No, it's my mom's."

Maggie smiled. "So, your mom's home?"

"I guess."

"Let's go inside," Maggie said. "I don't want to be out here anymore."

"Okay."

They ran along the front walk but stopped dead in their tracks. The front door stood wide open with blood smears all down it. Perched on the roof of the garage, just over the front door, was a crow which stared down at them with something bloody hanging from its beak.

"Mom?" Peter yelled out. He left Maggie standing on the walk as he raced to the front door.

"Stop," Maggie yelled out but Peter didn't listen.

Peter burst through the front door. "Mom? Dad?" He ran through the living room and the dining room and then into the kitchen.

No one was there.

Peter heard Maggie calling him from outside but ignored her. He poked his head around the basement door and called out, "Mom?"

No one answered.

He turned to look upstairs.

Peter grabbed hold of the railing and slowly walked up the stairs toward the bedrooms. As he got closer, he thought he heard the sound of something ripping. "Mom?" he called out.

Still no answer.

He climbed further up the stairs. Along with the ripping, came a new sound, the sound of smacking. Peter found himself holding his breath.

He tried to remain calm as he inched up the stairs afraid of what he might find.

At the top of the stairs, he stopped and listened. Someone was definitely in his parents' bedroom. He was too afraid to call out so he quietly walked to the entrance and peeked in.

An old man, who Peter recognized as the guy who walked the giant poodle from down the street, sat on his parents' bed, his hands and face covered with blood and guts. Peter tore his eyes away from the man and looked down at the bed. A naked man and woman lay beside each other, both with their insides ripped out and spread out along the once white mattress. Peter recognized his mom's blond hair even though it looked pinkish in all the blood.

Peter thought he was going to puke.

The old man's head snapped up as Peter gagged. Their eyes met and Peter thought the old man smiled at him.

Peter stood frozen, unable to move.

The old man broke eye contact with Peter and dug into the woman's belly. Peter sagged to the floor. His mom and dad were dead, he now realized.

"Peter," Maggie screamed at the top of her lungs.

He snapped back to life. Peter jumped up and slammed the bedroom door shut and ran down the stairs a few steps at a time.

"Peter," Maggie yelled again.

"I'm coming," Peter yelled back. Maybe Maggie's parents could help them, he thought as he raced for the front door. They were their only hope now because Peter didn't want to be a big boy anymore.

The screen door flew open as Peter practically stumbled out onto the front lawn. Maggie ran to him and scooted behind him.

Peter looked up and saw what her shouting had been about. Standing on the curb facing them were more than a dozen moaning crazy people.

"Let's go inside," Maggie pleaded.

Without taking his eyes off the moaning crowd in front of him, Peter said, "There's one inside too. It killed my parents."

"What are we going to do?" she asked as tears streamed down her face. Her body trembled from the sobs.

A few of the crazies started up the lawn towards them. They moved slowly as if maybe Peter and Maggie might be a danger to them. After a few of them started to move though, the others began to follow.

Peter and Maggie backed away.

"I'm scared," Maggie said.

Peter didn't take his eyes off the closing crazies. "Don't run," he told her. "Let's keep walking back, real slow. We'll try to get into the backyard. There's a path there that'll take us into the forest." Peter took her hand. "Maybe we can lose them in there."

"What if they chase us?" she asked. "I can't run as fast as you."

"Don't worry, I won't leave you, I promise."

They continued backwards and slowly turned to their left, aiming towards the side of the house.

All the crazies were in the yard now. Their eerie moans floated through the air like helium balloons.

Peter spun around when he heard the clink of metal hitting metal behind them.

The fence door to the backyard was open and more of the crazies were streaming through it.

Peter and Maggie were surrounded.

Peter looked quickly around for an escape route but there was none.

It was hopeless.

Peter felt tears welling in his eyes and felt sick to his stomach. He didn't want to die.

The sound of a roaring vehicle caught the crazies' attention. They turned away from Peter and Maggie.

Peter tugged Maggie closer to him. "When I say go, we're going to run for it, okay?"

"There's too many of them."

"We can't stay here."

Maggie looked up at him. "Let's run inside."

"I told you…" Before he could get the rest of the sentence out a large SUV flew over the curb and slammed directly into the crazies who stood there as if in a daze. The truck threw them into the air as if they weighed nothing.

Peter watched as one of the crazies fell under a wheel of the SUV. Its head pushed into the lawn until it disappeared from sight.

The truck stopped in the middle of the lawn, the front of it covered with blood and gore. Bodies of the crazies who had survived the impact writhed on the lawn, many of them missing arms and legs. Peter stood stunned, unable to move. The picture of that head being squished into the lawn burned into his mind.

"Get down," a woman's voice yelled.

Peter continued to stand there as if frozen in place. Maggie tugged at his arm as she screamed and screamed but Peter couldn't move.

"Get down," the woman yelled again.

A gunshot rang out and Peter hit the ground, dragging Maggie with him. Was he shot, he wondered? He suddenly felt numb.

More gunshots rang out over his head. He slid closer to Maggie and covered her as best he could with his body.

The gunshots seemed to Peter to go on for an eternity.

Peter felt a hand on his shoulder and he screamed.

"It's okay buddy. It's me," a man's voice told him.

The gunshots still rang in Peter's ears. He lifted his head and kneeling over him was his dad. Peter couldn't believe his eyes. He'd seen him dead upstairs. Could it have been a dream? Maybe he'd mistakenly eaten something with peanuts and had gone into shock.

"Are you hurt?" his dad asked him.

"I thought you were inside. I saw you…" Peter threw himself into his father's arms as tears streamed down his face.

Peter's dad held him and stroked his head as a female police officer picked up Maggie. "Who's your friend?" his dad asked.

"That's Maggie," he answered between sniffles.

The police officer approached them and Peter realized it was his aunt Sara. "Hi Petey," she said.

"Hi," was all Peter could get out.

"So, what did you mean, you saw me inside?" his dad asked.

Peter wiped away his tears with the back of his arm. "Upstairs, in your bedroom." He began to cry again.

"It's okay buddy, shhh." He held his son tight. "You've been through a lot but I'm here now. It was just your imagination playing tricks on you."

Peter pushed himself away. "No, it wasn't my imagination. I saw Mommy up there and she was naked and all eaten up, and, and, there was a man with her on the bed and I thought it was you."

"Was it one of the moaners?" his dad asked.

Peter seemed confused for a moment but realized what his father meant. "No, it was a real man but there was a crazy guy up there too and he was eating them." Peter's face scrunched up and tears flowed freely down it. Bawling now, Peter said through trembling lips, "I thought it was you."

"Bitch," Peter's dad suddenly cursed. He looked to his sister. "I have to see for myself."

"What does it matter?" Sara asked.

"I have to know."

Sara put Peter and Maggie in the police truck. "Don't worry," she said, "we'll be right back. The windows are shatterproof so no one can get in. Just don't leave the truck, okay?"

Peter and Maggie both nodded.

"We won't be long," Sara told them. "As soon as we get back, we'll go find someplace safe, okay?"

Peter and Maggie nodded again.

"I want to see my mommy and daddy," Maggie said.

"You will," Sara said. "We'll all find them together, how's that?"

Maggie tried to smile.

"Remember, don't leave the truck and keep the doors locked."

Peter and Maggie watched as Peter's dad and his aunt disappeared into the house.

Maggie reached over and took Peter's hand. "Thanks for staying with me," she said.

"You're welcome." Peter gave her hand a light squeeze.

Several gunshots went off inside the house, making Peter and Maggie jump. The two of them stared at the front door in expectation.

Maggie let go of his hand. "Where are they?"

"I don't know."

"What should we do?" Maggie asked.

"Just wait I guess."

And so, they waited.

SQUEALER

Carl lay on his bed and stared at the ceiling. Long dark shadows crept along it as if fingers stretching out to grab him. He rolled over on his side and looked at his clock. It read 2:30 in the morning.

He heard his sister stir in the bed next to him. Probably dreaming about ponies, he guessed. He hated sharing a room with her. Why couldn't he have his own room like his friends, he'd asked his mom a million times?

That would never happen though. Ever since his dad had disappeared, they'd been living in smaller and smaller places as Mom tried to make ends meet.

Carl quietly pulled the bed covers down and slid into a sitting position at the edge of the bed. He stared at his sister for a moment to see if she was still asleep. Confident she was, he eased himself out of bed and walked to a chair in the corner of the room where he'd thrown his clothes earlier. The room was dark except for the stupid night light his sister made them use. He stood in front of the chair until his eyes adjusted to the darkness and then carefully took his pajamas off and put on his clothes.

His sister Cheryl moved in her bed and Carl froze. He was fifteen years old and needed his privacy. Not only did he hate sharing a bedroom with her, he hated her. He also hated all the stupid stuffed animals she had. It reminded him how bad he wanted a real pet but his mom had said they couldn't afford one.

The room grew quiet again as Carl finished putting on his clothes and kept a watchful eye on his sister. Once he had everything on, he pulled a backpack from under his bed and draped it over his shoulder. As he approached the bedroom door, he heard a voice he knew only too well.

"Where are you going?" his sister asked.

Carl froze in his tracks and gritted his teeth. He turned around but could barely make her out in the darkness. He crept back into the room. "Go back to sleep."

"I want to know where you're going," she demanded.

"It's none of your business."

Cheryl pulled herself into a sitting position. "I'll tell Mom."

"Why are you such a little shit?"

"And I'm going to tell her you said a bad word."

Carl felt himself tremble inside. No one could get him worked up like her. His eyes had adjusted to the light and he could see the stupid smirk on her face. "What's it to you?"

"Cause I want to know," she said.

"I'm going out."

"Outside?" she asked as if it was the strangest thing in the world.

"No, out in the hall, stupid."

"Don't call me that."

"Or what? Let me guess, you're going to tell Mom." Carl grinned when he saw the stupid look on her face.

"That's right," she finally said.

Carl's grin faded. He thought for a moment about how he should handle this but quickly decided he had no choice; he'd just tell her. "Yes, I'm going outside."

"What for?" She pulled herself onto her knees and moved closer as if ready to share some big secret.

"If I tell you, you promise you won't say anything to anyone?"

"I promise." She eased closer.

"You know about all those pets that have gone missing?"

"Yeah."

Carl turned around as if to make sure there was no one else in the room listening. "Well, I heard some kids at school say that they saw old man Wilkinson dragging a dog into Mystery Forest."

"How come?" she asked, wide-eyed.

"No one knows," he answered. "Some of the kids think he's using them for sacrifices."

"What's sacrifices?" she asked.

Carl sat on the bed beside her. "It's when people kill other living things for favors."

Cheryl's face scrunched up like she'd smelled a bad fart. "You're lying."

"No, it's the truth."

"So, what are you going to do?"

Carl stood up and looked down at his sister. "I'm going to try to save one of them," he told her. "I've always wanted a pet but Mom says we can't afford one. Well, if I save one from being sacrificed, I should be allowed to keep it. Hey, maybe if I save a bunch of them, I'll even be in the paper and I'll be a hero and maybe we can move into a better place."

"I want to come."

Carl stared at her with disgust. "You can't."

"I'm gonna tell then."

Carl leaned towards her. "You're only ten," he told her. "It's too late for you to be out."

Cheryl looked at the clock. "It's past your bedtime too," she said. "If you don't take me, then I'm going to tell Mom."

Carl sighed. "Fine, but don't say I didn't warn you," he told her. "It could be dangerous and I may not be able to protect you."

"I'll be okay."

"Get dressed then," he said. "But if you get scared out there, I'm not bringing you back."

Cheryl hopped out of bed. "I won't be scared."

"We'll see," he said.

"I have to go to the bathroom," Cheryl informed him as they entered the forest.

"Can't you hold it?" he asked.

"No," she whined in the way that grated Carl so much.

"Go then," he said. "But make it snappy."

"Don't peek or try to scare me."

"Just go or I'm going to leave you out here."

She took a few steps off the path and stopped. "It's pretty dark."

"Of course, it's dark," he said. "It's the middle of the night and we're in a forest."

Cheryl seemed unsure what to do. "I don't know."

"I knew I shouldn't have brought you."

Cheryl walked back towards him. "I want to go home."

Carl pointed in the direction of their house. "It's that way."

"You have to come with me."

"No."

Cheryl crossed her arms across her chest and stood defiantly in front of her brother. "Then I'm going to tell."

"Go ahead," he said. "I can't wait to hear you explain what you were doing out here in the middle of the night."

Cheryl frowned.

It seemed to Carl that this was the first time he'd seen her stuck for something to say. "Well?" he taunted her.

She looked unsure but managed to get up the courage to storm into the bushes. "You better not leave while I'm going pee."

Carl waited.

They'd called it Mystery Forest ever since he was a kid. Legend had it that people had disappeared in the forest without a trace. Others said you could hear strange voices at night. Carl couldn't remember anyone disappearing in his lifetime other than his dad but that wasn't such a bad thing. Carl hated the way his dad had hurt his mom, both physically and mentally and was happy to see him gone. Actually, until the neighborhood pets started to disappear, stories about the forest had all but been forgotten.

The wind picked up and Carl began to imagine he heard strange sounds as he waited for his sister to finish her business. The branches of the dark pines hung menacingly above him, almost seemingly alive, as if just waiting for him to make a wrong move so they could grab him.

Carl began to pace nervously as he waited for his sister. The fallen pine needles crunched beneath his feet.

The snap of a breaking twig behind him caught his attention and he spun around. "Cheryl?"

There was no answer.

Carl looked through the thick darkness in the direction his sister had gone but he couldn't see a thing. He walked off the path and into the brush for a better look. "Cheryl," he called out again but got no reply. Stupid, stupid, stupid, he thought. Why did I let her come? He backed up until he was back on the path. What should he do now, he wondered?

A scream broke the silence around him.

"Cheryl?" he yelled.

A loud crack sounded in the darkness, followed by the sound of something crashing through the forest towards him. His heart pounding, Carl tried desperately to see what it was but he couldn't in the darkness. He backed away, down the dirt path, keeping an eye out for whatever it was. He imagined ugly, gnarled trees uprooting and crashing towards him.

Cheryl burst out of the darkness and fell onto the path a few yards from where Carl stood. Carl didn't move but watched as Cheryl lay on the ground motionless.

He looked around but couldn't see or hear anything. When he felt there was no immediate danger, he inched towards her, being careful to make as little sound as possible. As he approached her, he could hear her sobs.

"Cheryl?" he whispered.

She continued to sob. He stood beside her and took a quick look around, just to be safe. When he felt the coast was clear he knelt beside her and put his hand on her shoulder and shook it. "Cheryl," he said.

Cheryl looked up. Dirt covered her face along with streaks of tears. "Where were you?" Her mouth opened wide as she gulped for air as if she were a fish out of water.

"I was right here," he said. "Didn't you hear me calling you?"

"No," she answered between gulps of air.

Carl looked at her with disdain. He knew she was a lazy, pudgy brat but he'd never noticed just how out of shape she was. What a waste of space, he thought to himself. Why he'd let her come along he'd never know. "Stop blubbering," he told her.

"I hate you," she said.

"Well, I hate you more so get off your fat ass and stand up."

Cheryl didn't stand up but she did sit up. Carl noticed her shirt was ripped. "What happened to you anyway?"

"Something touched me."

"Touched you?"

She took a few more gulps of air. "In the dark," she said. "Something touched me."

"Where," he asked.

She touched the part of her shirt which was ripped. "Right here."

"It was probably a branch," he suggested. "Did you see any-one?"

"No, but that doesn't mean there wasn't anyone there."

"It was just a branch," he said. "Let's go."

Cheryl stood up defiantly and glared at him. "I'm not going anywhere."

"Fine, then stay here by yourself." He began to walk away.

"You're going to take me home, now," she ordered.

Carl spun around and walked briskly back to his sister. He shoved a finger towards the bridge of her nose. "No, I'm not," he told her. "I told you to stay home but you had to come. Everything has to be your way but not this time."

Cheryl smiled. Carl imagined that nothing made her happier than to get under his skin. "Lose the smile or lose your teeth," he said.

She continued to smile. "You're going to be in so much trouble when mom finds out how you kidnapped me and dragged me into the woods in the middle of the night."

"This was your idea, remember?"

"I don't care."

"Well, I don't care either. So, do what you want," he told her. "Either come with me or you can go back on your own." He paused and it was his turn to smile. "Through the dark woods, alone." With that, he turned and walked away. At first, she didn't say a word and Carl wondered, as he continued on, if she had begun to walk home alone.

Her wail broke the silence of the night. "Carl," she screamed. "Come back here right now."

Carl continued to walk not bothering to turn around. He heard the pattering of her feet coming up behind him. As she approached, he heard her gulping for air and he shook his head. "You should exercise more," he told her without looking back. "A ten-year-old girl shouldn't be as fat and out of shape as you are."

Cheryl finally caught up. "Mom says, I'm big-boned."

"You're big all right."

"Do you even know where you're going?" she asked.

"Yes," he said. He stopped suddenly and Cheryl crashed into the back of him. Carl turned to look at her. "I don't understand why you always have to follow me around. Why did you even want to come out here tonight? Is it just to bother me?"

Cheryl smiled again.

"What?" he asked.

"I just like being with you."

"Bullshit. You do it because you know it drives me crazy," he said. "Everything you do is an attempt to bother me. When I'm playing a game, you have to play it. If I'm going to a movie you have to come. When I get phone calls, you listen in. You really have to get a life," he told her.

"I hate you," she said.

"You already told me," he said. Tired of the conversation he turned away and continued down the path. Cheryl fell in behind him and followed along silently.

The clouds must have drifted because Carl realized for the first time that there was a full moon out. The moonlight streamed between the canopy of the trees overhead and cast strange shadows all around them. At least he could see better, he thought, despite the spooky setting.

They approached a fairly steep hill and Carl slowed his pace. He relished the fact that it would be a work out for his sister.

"Who's that?" Cheryl said, sounding frightened.

"Where?" Carl looked around but saw no one.

"At the top of the hill. Just off to the right. Look, he's staring right at us."

The thought of it made the hair on his arms prickle and he felt goosebumps rise on the back of his neck. For a moment he thought he saw someone looking down at them. It looked like an old man. Like old man Wilkinson to be exact.

A branch snapped up in the direction Cheryl was pointing. "There," she said.

Carl strained his eyes to see but couldn't see anyone.

Another branch snapped as if someone was headed their way.

"There's someone up there," she said. "I want to go home."

"Shhh," he said. Then in a whisper, he told her, "Let's move off the path into the forest and see what happens."

She grabbed onto his arm. "I don't want to go back into the forest."

"Just do it," he said. "If we hide in the dark, he won't be able to see us." Not waiting for her, he disappeared silently into the forest. He crouched down and waited. He didn't care if there was anyone else out there. He had a plan and he was sticking to it. There was no going back until it was completed. Cheryl approached him in the dark and sat down beside him but didn't say a word.

There were no more breaking branches but it seemed to Carl that the trees were whispering to each other. Did they know what he was up to? Would they try to stop him? He realized he was being stupid and that the darkness was only playing tricks with his mind. It should have been so simple. In and out, that was the plan but then his sister had to get involved.

They waited silently until Carl decided the coast was clear. He stood up and wiped away some old leaves and pine needles from his pants and looked around. "Coast's clear," he said.

"You sure," she asked.

"Pretty sure."

"When we get there," she said. "I get to pick."

"No," he said. "This is my plan and I get to pick the one I want."

"I want a cat," she said.

"I don't care what you want."

The two of them walked along the path and up the hill until they reached the top. Carl looked back the way they'd come and the forest seemed to disappear into the darkness. It was as if a thick, velvet curtain had been dropped at the bottom of the hill.

There was no turning back now.

As they walked along, the trees became denser, as if forcing the two of them to follow a path the trees had chosen. Carl also thought the forest looked different somehow, more menacing. Soon the path was so narrow they had to walk single file.

That's when the whispering started again.

"Did you hear that?" Carl asked.

"Stop it," she said.

"What?"

"You're trying to scare me."

"No, I'm not. Listen."

Cheryl tilted her head to listen.

"Hear it?"

"No. There's nothing."

Carl studied his sister's face. She wasn't smiling anymore but he knew she was lying. The trees were whispering again and he knew she'd heard it. "Come on, we have to go."

"What did you hear?" she asked.

"It doesn't matter."

The whispers grew louder and Carl thought he saw the trees moving. Not the ones beside the path but the ones deeper in the forest. It looked as if they were gliding along the forest floor, following them. He picked up the pace. He could tell Cheryl was scared because she wasn't her cocky self. Served her right, he thought. She deserved whatever she got.

He tried to block out the whispers.

They came to an intersection where two paths crossed. A hideously gnarled tree stood at one corner. The thick base was scarred with disease and its branches drooped down like a waterfall. Dark holes disappeared into its trunk. The thought that something valuable might be hidden in one of those holes occurred to Carl but he knew if he put his arm in one of them, he'd never get it back. An oily black sap oozed from the tree. This tree didn't whisper to him though.

"Are we lost?" Cheryl asked.

Carl ignored her as he continued to stare at the tree. High atop one of the many branches sat a crow that stared right back at him.

"What's the matter?" she asked.

Her question broke Carl from his thoughts and he pointed behind the tree. "Over there," he said.

"I'm not going in there."

"I can't leave you out here," he said. "What if that guy comes back?"

"There was no guy, stupid."

"What?" he asked.

Cheryl smiled that smile he hated so much. "I made it up because I wanted to go home but you're too stupid to take a hint."

"Fine, the joke's on me," he said. "Look, I don't want to leave you here in case something happens. If you come with me, I'll let you pick."

Cheryl seemed to have to think about this one. After a moment she said, "Okay, deal."

The two of them steered clear of the dying tree and walked into the forest. After a while, the trees began to thin and they came upon a clearing. The moon, now overhead, lit the area with its milky glow.

Cheryl spotted it first. Tied to the stump of a tree on a leash was a kitten. "It's a kitty," she said with a squeal. "And it's all mine and you can't ever touch it."

"But we found it together," he said.

"Tough luck." She didn't wait for Carl as she ran towards the kitten, her fat rump pulling at her stretchy pants. Carl watched her scoop up the kitten and start to pet it. "Help me free her," she demanded as Carl drew closer.

Cheryl pulled at the leash which was nailed to the stump. As Carl walked up beside her, she gave it one last tug. "You do it." She handed the leash to him as if he were her servant.

"Will we share it if I do?" he asked.

Cheryl hugged the kitten to her chest. "No, it's mine," she said. "But if you help me, I promise I won't tell mom that you went out tonight."

"Why don't you pick one of the other ones?" he asked.

"What other ones?" She looked around as if she might have missed them, and suddenly froze.

Her mouth dropped open and she flopped her fat ass onto the stump. All around her were the dead and mutilated bodies of the cats and dogs that had disappeared from the neighborhood. There were paws nailed to trees. Heads with their tongues sticking out hung from branches. Cheryl hadn't noticed in her haste to get to the kitten that surrounding them was a small wall of intestines and guts about two inches high.

"Did you hear me?" Carl asked, menacingly as he approached her. "Pick another one."

Cheryl stared at him. She must've been gripping the kitten too tightly because it hissed and scratched her. She let it drop and stared at the blood rising to the surface of her arm. "I don't understand," she finally managed to say.

"There's nothing to understand," he said. "I just do what the trees tell me to do."

"You did this?" she asked. "Why?"

Carl looked toward the trees as if waiting for them to answer and then turned back to her. "They helped me with a problem I had so in return I help them."

"Help them do what?"

"That's for me to know and for you to find out," he told her. "Isn't that what you always tell me?"

Cheryl stood up. "I'm going home and you're going to be in so much trouble when I tell Mom how crazy you are." She turned around and as she walked away, she gave Carl the finger. She didn't notice the axe leaning against the tree, which Carl picked up. He brought it swiftly down, across her neck, severing her head from her shoulders. He watched as her head plopped to the ground with a soft, wet, squishy sound.

Carl picked his sister's head up by the hair and carried it back to the deformed tree they'd come across earlier. He approached the tree, lifted the head up and unceremoniously dropped it into one of the dark holes.

"Say hi to Dad," he said.

UNDERNEATH THE STAIRS

"You're full of it," Tommy said to Kevin.

"No, I'm telling you, there's something under there," Kevin replied.

The two boys stood in Kevin's basement peering into the darkness behind the stairs that led up to the family room.

"I don't see anything," Tommy said. "Give me the hockey card."

"And you promise you won't hassle me anymore?" Kevin asked.

"That's what I said, didn't I?"

Kevin walked to the shelves on the other side of the basement. He moved aside the ugly painting of a crow that his mother had painted and opened a shoebox that contained his prized hockey card collection. He hesitantly took out the card Tommy wanted and walked back to where he waited.

"Here," he said, holding out the card.

Tommy looked at the card and smiled. He reached his pudgy hand out and grabbed it. "What's behind there anyway?" Tommy asked, looking back at the stairs.

"Just an unfinished storage area," Kevin said. "My dad said the builder tried to stick it to him by adding it in without asking."

"What did your dad do?"

"He told the guy he wasn't going to pay for it and that he could just fill it in for all he cared. It would've cost too much so the builder just left it unfinished and sealed it up."

"So, there's no way to get in there?"

"Nope. The only way in or out is if you squeeze through the spaces between the steps."

"Then how did it get in there?"

"That's the mystery."

"Anyone else ever see it?"

"Nope, just me."

"What's it look like?"

Kevin shrugged. "Can't tell, it's too dark back there."

"Then how do you know there's something even back there?"

"It tried to grab me once when I was going upstairs," Kevin explained, the scene still fresh in his mind. "That's why I always run up. Sometimes though I can see the whites of its eyes looking at me from under there."

"Well I don't see anything and this is stupid. I'm going home."

"Suit yourself. Just remember to run."

"Whatever," Tommy said, as he turned toward the stairs.

Kevin watched as Tommy waddled slowly up the stairs. He turned once, smiling at Kevin as if to show how stupid he thought the whole thing was. When Tommy reached the top step, Kevin drew a deep breath and sighed. Maybe it's not always under there, he thought.

Instead of going through the door, Tommy started back down the stairs, doing a lame victory dance. He waved the hockey card in the air, taunting Kevin. He made it the entire way to the bottom without incident.

"So much for your scary monster," he laughed. He turned and stomped back up the stairs.

Kevin felt dumb and wondered if the thing under the stairs had moved on. Suddenly, he saw glimmering eyes behind the stairs.

Tommy stopped halfway up the stairs, turned towards Kevin and gave him the finger. "You better have your lunch money ready tomorrow."

Kevin felt stupid, realizing he'd been tricked. "But you said…"

Two grisly hands popped out from behind the stairs and latched onto Tommy's ankles. The look of surprise on his face would have been funny if it wasn't for the situation. The hands yanked the boy's ankles back toward the darkness and Tommy fell forward, smashing his face against the bottom step.

Kevin saw blood spurt from Tommy's face.

Tommy dazed, lifted his head and looked up at Kevin, blood streaming down his face. His blank look caused Kevin to panic.

"Kick," Kevin yelled.

Suddenly, Tommy came alive. He thrashed about and tried desperately to hold onto one of the steps.

As his midsection slipped deeper into the darkness it suddenly became wedged. Kevin watched the rolls of fat bunch up tightly between the stairs.

Kevin heard the steps begin to creak under the pressure.

Tommy slowly lifted his bloodied face.

Kevin saw the fear in his eyes.

"Mommy," Tommy cried, just before his torso exploded in a gory mess and disappeared between the steps into the darkness.

Kevin heard the sickening sounds of gnashing teeth and meat being stripped from the bones. A sudden wave of nausea and panic swept through him as he dashed for the stairs. He stopped dead when he saw the greedy eyes staring at him.

"Well?" Kevin asked.

His hockey card flew out from behind the stairs and landed at his feet. Kevin picked it up and put it back into his shoebox. He slowly walked back to the stairs. "Thanks," he said.

Kevin waited until he heard Tommy's body being dragged deeper into the darkness. He sprinted up the stairs and closed the door behind him.

TYPO

Allan clicked away on his keyboard, his eyes glued to the computer screen. He moved from site to site along the endless highways of the internet oblivious to everything else around him.

At the age of thirty-five, Allan had only recently discovered the Dark Web and was in a hurry to catch up. He loved everything about it, especially the porn.

In his darkened basement with nothing but a glowing monitor for light, his fingers flew across the keyboard as visions of busty, naked blondes danced across his imagination. In his haste, he typed the wrong URL and instead of cute cheerleaders flashing up on his screen, he saw a black skull on a red background, its eye sockets glowing yellow.

Pissed off, he hit backspace but nothing changed. He tried control, alt, delete to get out of it, but still nothing. Allan reached for the power button to reboot his computer when the skull smiled at him with a wicked grin.

Spooked, he quickly turned off the computer, waited ten seconds and turned it back on. The screen came back to life but instead of the usual computer jargon scrolling across his screen, there was only the same grinning skull. He sat glumly staring at it, wondering what to do when it spoke to him.

"Would you like to come in?" it asked.

Allan fell back in his chair in surprise. After regaining his composure, he settled again into his chair and stared at the skull.

"Would you like to come in?" it asked again.

Allan waited, unsure what to do.

"We know you do," it added.

The skull's mouth began to open. A little bit at first but gradually wider and wider until suddenly its jaws slammed shut with a loud snap.

"We want you to join us," the voice said. "We have things to show you."

The initial scare worn off; Allan let his hand hover over the mouse nervously.

"Last chance," it said, raising goosebumps along the back of Allan's neck. The skull floated on the screen grinning; its glowing eyes subdued as if waiting for him to decide.

This is bullshit, he thought. It's only a web page.

He clicked on the skull and the eyes began to glow brighter and brighter until it let out a menacing laugh.

Panicked, Allan turned off the computer and again tried to reboot, but to his horror, the laughing skull reappeared.

"Welcome," it said. The skull began to bleed, dissolving into a bubbling mass of goo.

The screen went black.

A second later, an image of the outdoors appeared. It was as if he was looking through a camera lens. Whatever it was moved along some bushes until a small bungalow came into view. Allan's eyes followed its path into the backyard and then towards the house. He continued to follow it as it made its way to the back door of the bungalow. Allan watched as the door opened wide and it entered the house.

It moved slowly down a darkened hallway and into a room.

The drapes were not firmly shut in the room and the moon lent an eerie light to the scene. There appeared to be two people under the covers sleeping. The camera stood perfectly still for a moment as if studying the pair in the bed.

Without warning, the pair were attacked.

Allan sat horrified, his eyes glued to the screen. Screams and snarls assaulted his ears as blurred figures darted across his monitor.

"It's so realistic," he murmured, mesmerized by the chaotic scene.

The screams died away leaving only the sounds of thrashing on the bed and the sight of dark forms ripping the covers apart.

Finally, everything became quiet.

Allan didn't move but instead continued to stare at the screen.

The room suddenly lit up as if a flashbulb had gone off, exposing the grisly scene. Blood was splashed everywhere and lying in the bed were the remains of two bodies. The bodies were so badly mangled Allan couldn't tell if they were male or female. There was blood all over the bed, the floor, and the walls. Allan thought he even saw blood on the ceiling. The view panned over to the side of the bed where a severed arm lay lifeless on the floor.

The room went dark.

Allan's eyes stayed glued to the screen as the scene moved through the dark house and out the back door.

The transmission went dead.

The screen flickered for a moment and went back to its normal defaults. Once again Allan had control of his computer. He tried a couple of sites he knew by heart and found everything working again.

He didn't know what to make of it. Should he call the police? No need to do that, he decided. It obviously wasn't real and the last thing he wanted was to have the police going through his computer's history and seeing what kind of sites he visited. No, he'd just try to forget about it. He was about to log off when he received an e-mail from an address he didn't recognize.

He opened the e-mail anyway and found himself looking at a snapshot of the gory scene he'd just witnessed a moment ago. Trembling, he immediately deleted the e-mail and shut off the computer. He quickly walked up the stairs from his basement into the hallway above.

The house was deathly still and pitch black. He must have been down there longer than he'd thought.

As he turned on some lights, he thought he heard a sound in one of the bedrooms above. He stood very still as he held his breath, waiting to see if he would hear it again.

Nothing.

Allan forced himself to take several deep breaths. Once calm, he toured the house turning on lights and locking all the doors and windows. He didn't hear anything else out of the ordinary and decided it must have been his imagination.

Used to living alone and fending for himself he wasn't easily frightened, but the strangeness with his computer had unsettled him.

He walked to the kitchen but doubled back and turned on the television in the family room to add some background noise. A late-night talk show had started and it occurred to him just how late it was. He turned it to the news channel so he could watch the top stories while he ate.

He wandered back into the kitchen and opened the fridge only to find what he already knew. It was empty. He rummaged through his cupboards and found a long-forgotten can of spaghetti. He opened it up, plopped its contents into a pan, slid it onto the burner and turned on the heat. As he stirred the cooking spaghetti, he heard the opening tune for the news. He couldn't help but go have a look just in case there was something about what he'd seen on his computer.

There was nothing about it in any of the lead stories.

He turned up the sound before he walked back to the kitchen.

After he had something in his belly and not hearing anything further on the news, he felt much better. He decided what he'd witnessed was nothing more than some amateur filmmaker's sick project.

Yawning, Allan headed to bed with hopes of forgetting the whole thing.

The next day, after finishing up at the warehouse where he worked, Allan decided to go retro and pick up a couple of pornos to spice up his evening. After what had occurred the previous night, he didn't feel much like going back on his computer.

He picked up some Chinese food and after arriving home, crashed down into his favorite chair, pulled up the coffee table and spread his supper around him. He turned on the television to check what was on before he threw in his entertainment for the night and ended up at the news channel.

He munched away as he watched the news stories stream by in quick thirty-second bursts of information. He shoved a chicken ball into his mouth as an image of a small bungalow that looked very familiar appeared on the screen.

Too familiar.

He almost choked on the chicken ball when the reporter began talking about a grisly murder scene that had just been discovered.

"This is Gloria Van Der Blank, in Watten Township, where two mangled bodies were found in this house just an hour ago. We have not been allowed into the house but from the look of the officers on the scene, it must be horrendous."

Allan stared in disbelief.

"Police are asking anyone with information on this crime to contact them immediately," the reporter finished.

Allan found himself perspiring and sank back into his chair.

Glancing at the videotapes on top of the TV, he frowned. Suddenly, he wasn't interested in porn anymore. If the killers were real and could e-mail him, they could certainly find out where he lived.

Allan's mind raced as he tried to figure out what to do.

Allan knew what he wasn't going to do.

What he did on his computer was his business so he wasn't calling the cops.

He picked up his cold dinner and carried it to the kitchen where he sealed all the cartons and placed them into the fridge. He rinsed his cutlery in the sink and looked out the window into the backyard where he noticed it had started to get dark.

The night was coming, but was anything else, he wondered?

He shuddered and stood for a minute watching the shadows steadily creep across his lawn. He shut off the water, turned away from the window and walked back into the family room. He paced the floor trying to think what he should do. Was what he'd witnessed a one-time thing or was this the beginning of something else?

Depression sank into him like a lead weight. He thought about his life and how it consisted of long sessions alone in front of a television set and then, more recently, in front of a computer in his basement. It suddenly became all so clear. He realized he'd spent much of his life with no purpose, trying to avoid reality by living in a fantasy world of projected images on screens of glass. It was like an unreal window to the world. A world he'd made to suit his own selfish needs with nothing to offer in return. But now reality had found him and he couldn't hide from it any longer.

He marched downstairs to the basement with newfound purpose. If whoever they were thought they could yank him from the comfortable existence he'd made for himself, they had another thing coming.

As he waited for his computer to boot up, he decided to print up the e-mail they'd sent him from his Deleted folder. He'd just cross out his e-mail address and mail it to the police. Let them track the psychos down.

The grinning skull appeared on his screen.

A cold chill raced down his spine and his body shuddered.

"What the fuck do you want?" he asked the skull. There was, of course, no answer, just the constant bobbing of its head.

What was it waiting for? He tapped on his keyboard and mouse but nothing happened. He thought again of calling the police or unplugging the computer. He even contemplated taking an ax to it.

Glowing brightly, the skull began to laugh.

It was showtime.

Just like the night before, the skull dissolved into a gory mess and the screen went blank. Allan leaned forward and as he did, an outdoor scene appeared on the screen. It was dark and hard to make out, but eventually a car came into view. Allan saw smears of blood on its windows.

"Fuck," he said under his breath.

As it moved past the car, strange lights appeared off in the distance.

Red swirling lights. Police, Allan thought.

As the scene unfolded, a small convenience store came into view with a police car parked in front of it. A body was sprawled across the front windshield as a crow dipped its beak into the eye socket and gobbled its contents down. The car's red lights swirled into the night. Around to the rear, a second body lay mangled beyond any hope of identification. As the camera circled the police car, it turned to face the store.

The lights in the store were out except for the emergency lights which cast an eerie red glow onto everything. The camera went through the entrance and casually moved up and down the aisles. Blood smeared the floor and shelves but no bodies were visible. Allan shoved his face closer to the screen and strained to make things out. The camera turned and moved towards the exit.

Allan moved closer to the screen.

The camera backed slowly out the door and as it did it panned towards the ceiling.

Hanging in grotesque poses were close to half a dozen bodies. Allan couldn't tell if they were tied to the ceiling or if they'd been nailed there but whatever was holding them in place was doing its job. Allan strained for a better look but the doors abruptly slammed shut in front of the camera.

Once again it was on the move. Allan saw another store off in the distance, closing fast. As the camera passed a darkened storefront, there was no reflection in the plate glass window.

Where was the cameraman?

Then, as if it had read his mind, it stopped, backed up and slowly turned to face the glass window.

Allan held his breath.

There was nothing there.

He shuddered and the fear he felt intensified.

Allan wasn't sure how they did it but he tried to convince himself none of it was real. They were clever but everything had an answer and he was going to get to the bottom of it. Whatever it was though, it was on the move again.

He watched as it moved down an empty street. It stopped for a second to look at the street sign as if to get its bearing.

Allan watched, unable to pull himself away, as it covered block after block without a break or even a glance to the right or left. The thing was on a mission but what it was, only time would tell.

Finally, it stopped.

Once again, the view panned skyward towards a street sign. And to Allan's horror, it was the crossroads of his block.

He cursed himself for his stupidity. What the hell had he been thinking? He decided he'd waited long enough before calling the police. He reached for his phone but grabbed nothing but air.

He'd left the phone upstairs.

He pushed himself away from the computer and lifted himself from his chair. Just before he left the room something on the screen caught his eye.

From a driveway a man and a woman appeared, they turned onto the sidewalk and headed straight towards the camera. Allan stood frozen as he stared at the unfolding scene. As the couple got closer, Allan screamed at his computer, begging for the couple to look up, to run, to save themselves, but they seemed engrossed in conversation. Each step they took drew them closer to their savage end.

Ten steps, eight steps, six steps …

Why couldn't they see the horror before them, Allan wondered? He wanted to race outside to warn them but he realized it was too late. Unable to tear his gaze from the screen he watched as the couple drew closer.

The couple passed without incident.

Allan couldn't understand what happened. Why hadn't they been attacked? He kept his eyes glued to the screen expecting at any moment to see the camera turn back towards the couple and attack them, but it never did.

Allan continued to watch until finally the camera stopped and turned ever so slowly, as if for effect. It didn't have to though because Allan quickly realized where it was.

It was in front of his house.

Allan collapsed into his chair. In the dark basement with only the monitor's glow to give him light he struggled with what he should do. It was too late to try to escape, he concluded. He stared at the monitor hoping whatever it was out there would just pass by as it had with the couple.

The computer screen continued to show the front of his house. The view had not changed nor moved.

A woman's voice spoke to him through his speakers. "Ask us in, Allan," she said.

The voice startled him. It was the suddenness, not the voice that scared him. The voice had almost been reassuring in a way.

"Ask us in," she said again.

Allan watched the screen as his house grew closer. Whatever it was, it was in no hurry as it approached. The camera stopped before the front door and turned around taking in the view of the neighborhood as if giving Allan one last look.

Then it turned back towards the door.

"Ask us in," she said, more sternly now.

"No," he finally managed to scream.

The door opened as if on its own and it entered the house. Allan watched in horror as it crossed the main floor of his home.

He looked around frantically for an escape route or a weapon.

There was neither.

He watched as the thing moved through the different rooms upstairs as if searching for something.

It was in the kitchen now. It wouldn't be long until it found the basement stairs.

The door to the basement opened.

Allan started to shiver as he watched it move down the steps towards him.

It reached the bottom of the stairs, yet Allan hadn't heard a sound. He would have never known it was even there if he hadn't been watching it on his screen. He stared in disbelief as he saw himself finally appear on his monitor. He wondered if there were others out there on the internet, right now, watching him.

He swung his chair around to face the thing, but nothing was there. He looked out of the corner of his eye and noticed he was still on the screen, so he knew he wasn't alone.

"Get out of my house," he screamed.

Nothing happened.

"Did you hear me?" he said with more confidence this time. "Get out of my house." Allan was surprised to hear himself but it felt good. He'd never been assertive before.

The skull reappeared on the computer screen. "Good-bye Allan," it said, and the screen went dark.

The room went pitch black.

Unable to move, Allan braced himself for the attack. He thought he felt something brush against him and he jumped, banging himself against the computer desk.

He waited, unable to move.

After a few deep breaths, he slowly eased his way towards the light switch. He felt along the wall until he found it and after a moment of hesitation, he flipped it on.

The sudden shock from the lights blinded him for a moment. After his vision returned, he looked around but saw nothing suspicious.

Could it be that easy, he wondered? Was it meant to be some kind of life lesson? Something to help him change his ways? There had to be some kind of reason behind it. He decided he didn't want to stick around and find out.

He bolted from the room and raced up the stairs, taking them two at a time. As he rounded the corner into the kitchen, he felt a searing pain in his back and he dropped to the floor. He tried to get up but found himself unable to move.

Blood puddled beneath him and his back burned with pain.

As he lay motionless, he realized no one would miss him. It would probably be days or weeks before someone even bothered to come looking for him.

Allan felt himself drifting away, his life force bleeding out from beneath him. A tear dribbled down his cheek.

All because of a typo.

A NIGHT OUT

The bar stank of stale beer, sweat and sex. The heat inside was stifling but that didn't slow the frenetic gyrations of those on the dance floor. As the music thundered, the tightly packed crowd seemed almost in a trance. Glazed eyes stared at one another as they danced to the modern tribal beat.

Josh pressed himself tighter against Stacy, or was it Tracy? At the moment he didn't care. As he grabbed her ass, she surprised him by pulling off his shirt and throwing it into the crowd. She leaned forward, smiled a devilish grin and flicked his exposed nipples with her tongue.

Although he'd brought some roofies with him, which had come in handy many times before, he didn't think he'd be needing the drug tonight.

Josh's body glistened with sweat as he watched his dance partner practically giving him a bath with her tongue. The way she lapped at his chest and shoulders and neck reminded him of how his dog licked his hand over and over again for the salt.

He arched his neck back and stared at the ceiling as she worked her way down his body.

Small stars filled the ceiling making Josh dizzy. He couldn't figure out if they were painted on or just decals. Stringed lights in the shape of little red peppers bordered the ceiling and cast an eerie red glow across the stars. In the center of the ceiling, a large full moon hovered menacingly over him. It too was drenched in the blood-red glow of the lights. In the far corner sat what looked to Josh to be a jet black crow. It sat on its perch looking menacingly at the crowd and Josh wondered if it was real.

Somewhere in the crowd, someone screamed. Josh couldn't see who it was but the scream broke him from his trance-like gaze of the ceiling. He looked down at his dance partner who was now on her knees and smiled. She looked back at him. The intensity in her eyes flickered like flames.

She tugged at his belt.

Josh decided they'd better find a room.

As he reached to pull her up, a hand yanked his shoulder, spinning him around. In front of him stood his friend Mike. Behind Mike, supported by Drew and Chris was Bruce. Bruce looked as pale as ash but it was the blood dripping down his neck that caught Josh's attention.

"What the hell happened?" Josh asked, keeping his distance so he wouldn't get any blood on himself.

"We're getting the fuck out of here," Mike told him, looking over his shoulder as if something might be coming after him. "And here's your shirt." He tossed it to Josh.

"She bit me," Bruce said feebly as he held his hands against his wound.

Stacy, or Tracy, stood up nonchalantly and patted Josh on the ass. "I'm going to the bar for a drink," she said.

Surprised by her nonchalance, he only managed a nod as he watched her walk away.

He turned to Mike. "What the fuck is your problem?" he asked, "Take him to the john and clean him up."

Mike looked at him with disgust. "He's got a fucking gouge in his neck."

Bruce looked like he might pass out but he managed to say, "She bit me," again.

"I heard you the first time," Josh said as he approached him. "Let me have a look."

Bruce reluctantly pulled his hands away, revealing a nasty wound that seemed to pulse with every heartbeat.

Josh couldn't believe the look of the wound but put on a straight face. "It's not so bad," he said. "But I don't think we should move him until the bleeding stops. Find him a chair and let him sit down for a while."

Bruce regained some of his color. "Screw you. I'm getting out of here," he said. "This place is fucked."

"There's nothing wrong with this place, you pussy," Josh said as he put on his shirt.

Mike walked back to Bruce and put an arm around him to help prop him up. "We're taking him to Emergency," he said. "Are you coming or not?"

Josh looked towards the bar and spotted her. His mind raced with the different scenarios. If his friends left and he didn't score he was out taxi fare. If he did go, he might be missing the best sex he'd had in years.

"Forget her," Drew said. "She'll probably bite off something worse. We have to get Bruce to the hospital."

"All right, all right," Josh said. "Take him out to the car and I'll be there in a minute. I just have to say goodbye."

"You better not be fucking with us," Mike said. "You got two minutes and then we're gone."

"Give me one."

"You got it," Mike told him. "Don't let your pecker do your thinking for you." Mike gently turned Bruce around and the group of them disappeared into the crowd.

Josh ran his fingers through his hair as he let out a deep breath.

He'd decided what he had to do.

The crowd was tight with half-clad, sexually charged bodies. Josh pushed his way towards the bar, letting his hands brush against asses as he walked along. Get it where you can, he thought.

She stood at the bar, her skin glistening from the work out on the dance floor. As Josh approached, he saw her lift her face in the air. She seemed to sniff at it as if she'd smelled a fart and was trying to figure out who the culprit was. After one more sniff, she slowly turned her head and their eyes met.

"I thought I sensed you coming," she said.

"Sorry about my friends, they…" She put a finger to his lips.

"You have to go," she said.

"What?" Josh felt the anger rise inside him. If this bitch thought she could just blow him off after her little tease session, she had another thing coming. He kept up his smile despite his venomous thoughts. "You mean we have to go, right?"

"No, just you. I can't explain," she said. "Just trust me that you should leave. Now."

He reached into his pants pocket and fingered the package of a powdery substance, the one he kept for moments like these. He cupped his hand around it and casually pulled it from his pocket.

"But my friends are gone," he lied. "I thought we had something going so I told them to go ahead."

She smiled. "We do," she said. "That's why you have to go. Please, you just have to trust me."

He studied her face. She was stunning. Her long brown hair and those dark eyes. The kind of dark that hides their true color. When he looked at her in a certain way her eyes seemed almost red. And her teeth were whiter than any he'd seen before. He had a thing for white teeth. Call it a fetish if you will. They were a bit more jagged than he liked but nothing a good filing couldn't fix.

"How will I get home?" he asked.

She didn't answer. She seemed nervous and preoccupied. The idea that there might be a boyfriend involved in all this crossed his mind. She began to look around the bar in a way that only added credence to his theory. He used her distraction to drop the drug quickly into her drink.

"I'll make you a deal," he said after he finished pouring the roofie into her drink. "Walk me to a cab and give me your number. Or better yet, give me a drive home and I'll go."

She thought about this for a moment and agreed. She grabbed for her glass and with a couple of large gulps, drained her drink.

Things couldn't be going better, he thought.

She grabbed his hand and he was surprised by how strong her grip was. She gave him a tug that nearly lifted him from his feet and they were off.

"What's the big hurry?" he asked, trying to keep up.

She looked up at the clock above the front doors of the bar. It was only a few minutes before midnight. She gave him another tug.

As she yanked him through the crowd, Josh noticed a couple of gigantic bouncer types suddenly appear in front of the doors as if to bar their exit. Josh had a sudden feeling that something wasn't right.

He tried to pull away but her grip held firm. Had they seen him spike her drink, he wondered? Perspiration ran down his back and he felt scared for the first time in quite a while.

"Open the doors," she yelled over the din of the crowd.

The bouncers didn't move.

At the speed they were going, Josh feared they might crash headfirst into the doors but at the last moment, the bouncers threw them open. She gave another yank and Josh felt himself lift off the ground and fly through the open doors. As he crashed to the ground outside the bar, he thought he heard the clock strike midnight. At first, he thought the bonging was in his head. A side effect from his crash landing. After the twelfth bong, the doors to the bar slammed shut and Josh knew it wasn't in his head.

He laid there stunned.

Everything seemed eerily quiet.

Then the screaming started.

"Get up," she said, her voice starting to sound slurred.

Josh sat up. "What the hell's going on?"

"We have to go," she ordered, "Now."

Horrible screams filled the air. Josh turned to look at the bar. He felt her tight grip around his arm again. Before he knew it, he was back on his feet.

"What's going on in there?" he asked, staring at the bar as she pulled him away.

"Nothing you want to see," she said.

The bar's lights went out.

"Run," she said.

They hadn't made it half a block when the doors to the bar burst open. A young woman ran screaming from the doorway and into the street, behind her a guy built like a football player quickly followed. Her boyfriend, Josh guessed. The boyfriend seemed to have something in a headlock.

From where Josh stood it looked like the boyfriend was fighting with a large dog. The girlfriend spotted Josh and turned to face him.

"Help us," she screamed.

Josh stood in horror as a dark hairy figure shot out from the bar like a rocket and attacked the girl. A fountain of blood spewed from her ravaged neck.

Josh couldn't move.

"You can't help them," his date said, once again tugging at his arm.

Instincts kicked in and Josh didn't need anyone tugging at him anymore. The two of them ran until he couldn't run any further.

Josh bent over, clutching his sides as he drew in deep gulps of air. Each breath sent a new stitch of pain up his side. He lifted his head and looked around. Fucking bikers, he thought. He'd heard about bikers using dogs to settle scores. It was a new tactic they used to put fear into those who didn't fall in line. At least that's what he wanted to believe.

He straightened up and took a quick look around. The coast looked clear. Josh let out a sigh of relief but wondered how she'd known something was going down. He turned to ask her that very question when he noticed her doubled over in pain. Shouldn't have drunk my potion so fast, he thought to himself, clearly satisfied with how things were turning out.

"It's too late," she said, clutching her belly. With trembling hands, she reached into a pocket and brought out a set of keys. "Take my car," she said. "It's the red one right over there." She nodded her head towards a parked sports car down the road." She tossed the keys to him and they dropped by his feet.

Josh picked up the keys. "Are you okay?" he asked, trying his best to sound concerned.

"I'm changing," she seemed to growl. "Run."

You're changing all right, he thought to himself. He walked over to her and put an arm around her as he checked the area for possible witnesses. He helped her walk into the dark shadows of the closest alley, whispering soothing words of comfort to her. It wasn't his preferred choice of setting but sex was sex.

He laid her down on the ground and began to undo his belt.

She tried to get up but collapsed to the ground with a grunt. "What did you do?" she asked pathetically. Her back arched as if she'd landed on a rock. "You stupid, stupid man."

We'll see who's the stupid one, he told himself.

Slurring her words badly she said, "I liked you. I wanted to protect you."

"Thanks, honey," he answered. "I appreciate your gesture but you're of more use to me like this." He unzipped his pants and let them slip down to his ankles, his erection proudly showing in the dim light.

"I can't change," she said.

"No worries there," he told her. He bent down and reached for her top.

"If I can't change, I can't protect you."

Smiling, Josh showed her the rubber he had ready. "It's okay, I brought my own protection."

As he peeled off her top, her hand sprang up and grabbed his wrist. Surprised, he looked at it and noticed the patches of hair that had magically appeared on her arm and hand. Where the fuck did that come from? He pulled away in disgust. Her grip loosened and her arm fell to the ground.

The drug had finally put her under.

The sight of the hair had surprised him. Why hadn't he noticed it before and what other surprises had she kept from him? He wasn't going to let a little setback slow him down though. He climbed on top of her and leaned in for a kiss but stopped and stared at her in confusion. Her face was covered in hair and those pearly white teeth he'd so admired earlier now seemed more like fangs than teeth.

Josh jumped to his feet. His erection now gone south. "What the fuck," he muttered.

A deep growl sounded behind him.

Slowly, Josh turned. His pants still hung around his ankles.

Standing at the edge of the alley were things you only saw at the movies.

Three large, hulking werewolves left the light of the street, entered the darkness of the alley and moved menacingly towards him.

Josh stood frozen in terror, unable to scream, his flaccid penis pointing at the pants around his ankles.

And in the dim light of the alleyway, the last thing Josh saw was their oh so white teeth.

ACID RAIN

The three of us began the long walk back to our hotel. The breeze had died down but dark sinister looking clouds hung menacingly overhead.

"I don't think we're going to make it back to the hotel before those clouds open up on us," I commented.

"What do you want to do?" My wife Heather asked, looking up at the clouds to see for herself.

"I don't know. Keep walking?" I said. "A bit of rain never killed anyone."

The sounds of screaming, far off in the distance, caught our attention.

"What's that Mommy?" Our daughter Katlyn asked.

Heather strained her eyes in the direction of the screams. "I don't know Honey, maybe there was an accident." Something off in the distance caught her eye. "Do you see that, Rob? What is it?"

"I'm not sure."

Heather appeared to be about to ask something when more screams, much closer this time, filled the air.

"Mommy, I'm scared."

"It's okay, Mommy and Daddy are here."

"I want to go back to the hotel," Katlyn said, already pulling at her mother's arm.

"Can you tell where the screaming is coming from?" Heather asked.

"No, but it's stopped again. Think we should check it out?"

"No." She said abruptly.

"Maybe someone needs help," I said.

"I don't care. Let's go find some shelter. I don't like the look of those clouds."

"Okay boss, where to?"

"Look, over there." Heather pointed. "It's one of those tourist bus shelters. Why don't we ride out the storm in there?"

Without another word we both grabbed Katlyn's hands and walked toward the shelter. Overhead hundreds of crows quickly flew by as if they also wanted to escape the oncoming storm.

That's when the screaming began in earnest. Without looking back, the three of us raced toward the shelter, not wanting to know what was going on behind us. As we ran, our surroundings darkened.

The rain was closing in.

The screaming seemed all around us as we ducked into the shelter. We were the only ones there but we could see others in the distance making their way toward us.

"What is that racket?" a voice inquired, startling the three of us.

I turned around and noticed an older woman behind a glass partition. Above her, a sign read Bus Tour Tickets.

"You work here?" I asked?

"Yes sir. Going to buy some tickets?" the woman asked.

"No thanks. We're just trying to ride out the storm."

"Sorry, this shelter is just for…" But before she could get the rest out, the sickening sound of frantic screams echoed through the shelter. The ticket woman opened the door to her booth and stepped out into the waiting room just as a couple of teenage girls came scurrying in.

"Does anyone know what's going on?" one of the girls asked as she played with her phone. "I can't get any reception on my phone."

"Me either," her friend said looking frustrated.

I checked my phone and it wasn't picking up a signal either.

The screaming stopped again, just as suddenly as it began.

The six of us turned and stared out toward the great wall of rain. The moisture in the air was increasing as the wall of rain moved closer. All of us had our phones out.

"The storm must be interfering with our phones somehow," I said.

"Have you ever seen anything like this?" the ticket woman asked.

We shrugged.

"I think the screams are coming from inside the rain," one of the girls said.

"Maybe the rain's really cold," Katlyn offered.

Everyone seemed pleased with that explanation.

"That could be," the other girl piped in hopefully.

"Can anyone make out what's going on over there?" Heather asked. "It's too far for me to see anything."

"Not me. It must still be about seven or eight blocks away," I answered.

"Hold on a second," the ticket lady said as she turned back to her booth. "I think I've got some binoculars back there somewhere."

I picked Katlyn up and walked over to some benches. Heather stayed where she was, hypnotized by the wall of rain headed our way.

"You okay?" I asked Katlyn, giving her a reassuring hug.

"I'm okay. We're safe in here, right?"

"You betcha."

The ticket lady came back with a pair of ancient-looking binoculars in her chubby hands. "I knew I had them in there somewhere," she said proudly.

"Can you make out anything?" one of the girls asked.

The ticket lady put the binoculars to her eyes and peered out towards the oncoming storm. Her fat fingers played with the focus gizmo as she muttered something under her breath.

"What is it?" I asked. "What do you see?" I started to grow impatient with her constant fiddling and lack of information. I got up and stepped toward her as the binoculars slowly dropped from her face. She looked pale and her hands shook. I reached for the binoculars just as they slipped from her hands, crashing to the cement floor.

"Impossible," she whispered.

I snapped up the binoculars and examined them for damage. When I saw they were still in good shape I raised them to my eyes. I stood motionless as I looked toward the wall of rain. I too began to fidget with the focus, not believing what I was seeing.

"Rob?" Heather said.

I didn't answer but instead played frantically with the focus.

"Rob." She tried again. "Tell us what you see."

"Let me see, Daddy," Katlyn asked.

Screams filled the air. Horrible, grotesque, terrified screams.

"I'm scared," one of the teenage girls confided to her friend.

More screams.

"It's the rain," I said, to no one in particular.

The sound of sobbing filled the shelter. I turned toward the sobbing and saw the ticket lady huddled against the Plexiglas wall crying.

"What's happening, Rob? Say something," Heather pleaded.

"It's the rain," I said again. My voice sounded empty.

"What about the rain? For God sakes, tell us what's going on."

I lifted the binoculars again to have another look as if what I'd seen must have been a mistake. After staring off toward the rain for a moment I brought the binoculars back down.

"What did you see?" one of the teenage girls begged.

"The rain... It's melting them."

"Melting who? What are you saying?" Heather asked.

Heather finally took the binoculars for herself as I stood there dumbfounded.

"We have to get out of here," she said, dropping the binoculars.

A man suddenly lurched into the shelter collapsing to the hard cement floor. Everyone jumped in surprise as the two teenage girls screamed. Smoke drifted off his body and stank up the shelter. I broke from my trance and quickly knelt beside the man.

"You okay?" I asked as I turned the man over. The man's face was burned and skin hung off him like melted wax. I felt bile rise in my throat.

Screaming, the two teenage girls ran from the shelter in hysterics.

"Wait, come back. You're running toward it," I shouted, but it was no use. They didn't care or didn't hear me as they ran blindly from the horror they'd just witnessed.

"Stop them, Robert," my wife begged me.

"It's too late," I answered, as I picked up the binoculars and placed them back to my eyes. My heart pounded in my chest as if it was getting ready to burst right out of it. I watched in horror as the two girls ran wildly down the street.

A splattering of rain hit them and I watched helplessly as the two girls danced in sick twisted movements, their arms flailing around as if to ward off whatever was attacking them.

I continued to watch the gruesome display as the two girls collapsed to the ground, writhing in pain. It was only seconds later, when the rain was fully on them, that the screams started in earnest.

I watched as their young flesh melted away.

Unexpectantly, one of the girls managed to crawl to her feet and began to slowly stumble back towards the shelter, her arms stretched out as if wanting a hug. The rain beat down on her harder and her clothes gave way, leaving nothing but a badly burned walking corpse.

The girl made it only a few more steps before her body finally gave way from under her.

I pulled the binoculars away from my face. I'd had enough.

"He's dead," Heather proclaimed, startling me.

"What?"

"The man's dead," she repeated, kneeling beside the man who'd staggered in earlier.

I dragged the body off to the side and draped it with my jacket.

"Is this really happening?" the ticket lady asked, as she pulled herself to her feet.

"Yes," I replied, not even bothering to make eye contact.

"We have to get Katlyn out of here," Heather said.

"To where?" I asked. "And end up like those two?" I motioned toward the girls. "We should stay put. Ride it out."

"For God's sake, there's no door here. The rain will easily reach us."

"Not if we get to the back and stand on the benches."

"But we could run in the opposite direction. Get somewhere with more protection."

"We can't risk it. We have no idea how fast the storm can move. We might only get a few hundred steps before it's on us."

The four of us stood quietly staring out toward the oncoming rain, no one saying a word. The rain was only a couple of blocks away now and closing fast. Heather latched on to Katlyn and held her tightly. The ticket lady sat slumped, head down, on one of the benches, crying. I stood by the doorway staring intensely at this freak of nature and tried desperately to come up with a way to save us all.

Gusts of wind blew into the shelter as droplets of the deadly rain started landing closer. As the rain slowly made its way towards us, the ugly smell of acidity began to permeate the shelter.

From high above, the clouds, instead of being dark and menacing, took on a pleasant pinkish hue and rolled gently across the sky.

But still it came.

The sound of rain hitting the roof of our shelter marked the arrival of the storm at our doorstep. The ticket lady began to scream hysterically.

"Stop it. You're scaring my child," Heather bellowed at the woman, tightening her grip on Katlyn as if to protect her somehow from this crazy woman's screams.

I rushed over to the woman, now crumpled in a fetal position and tried to comfort her as best I could. "It'll be okay. We're all safe in here and once the storm passes, we can go find help." I awkwardly tried to hold her in an attempt to comfort her but she pushed me away.

"We're never getting out of here. We're going to end up just like the rest of them," she bawled.

"Make her stop," Heather begged.

Would we make it out of this nightmare, I wondered? I turned my attention back to the ticket lady who had stopped crying and was now dragging herself pitifully along the ground toward the back of the shelter.

"What do you think we should do?" Heather asked.

"I don't know," I answered honestly.

"Come over here and sit with us then. Katlyn wants you to sit with her."

I looked over my shoulder toward the shelter's entrance and noticed the rainwater starting to pool. So far it hadn't made its way in, but it was only a matter of time if this heavy downpour kept up.

I placed a hand against one of the Plexiglas walls and it was warm to the touch. I decided not to mention it and casually walked toward my wife and daughter. I sat beside Katlyn and put my arm around her. I rested my other hand on my wife's thigh and gave it a comforting squeeze. She looked at me and I could see in her eyes, she was afraid. I tried to smile reassuringly.

A few hours passed with no sign of the rain letting up. If anything, the rain came down harder than before. We had no visibility outside the shelter as the storm directed all its fury at us.

The ticket lady hadn't spoken a word since her earlier outbreak. She sat huddled against the back corner, opposite us. Her eyes stared off into space, absent of any spark of emotion. I started to wonder if perhaps she'd snapped mentally and hoped she wouldn't cause trouble for us later.

Of course, we had bigger problems to worry about.

About an hour earlier the rainwater had started to make its way into our shelter. A little bit at first but it continued steadily until it covered almost one half of the shelter floor. We had watched in horror as the dead man's body, who I'd placed off to the side earlier, began to dissolve before our eyes. Mercifully the current dragged his body out of the shelter. There was about a six-foot gap now between us and the water. I found a discarded newspaper under one of the benches and threw it onto the water to see what would happen. It sizzled immediately and disintegrated to nothing in seconds.

"I hate not knowing what's going on out there," Heather said. "Is this happening everywhere or is it just on top of us?"

"I wish I knew," I answered, as I peered out into the rain. I placed one of my hands against the wall to test it again and found it hotter than before. "I was thinking, what if we covered Katlyn up as best we can and I carry her in my arms and race over to the restaurant we passed earlier?"

"Are you nuts? You're not taking her anywhere and you're not going anywhere either," she said, sounding scared.

I wanted to tell her about my fears of the shelter melting away around us and how the walls had been gradually getting hotter, but I saw no benefit in doing it so I kept my mouth shut.

A loud metallic snap followed by the sound of a splash caught my attention and made me almost jump out of my skin. The legs of one of the benches closest to the entrance had collapsed after being slowly melted away. When the bench finally collapsed to the floor, an acidic foam frothed around it as it began to dissolve.

"Get Katlyn onto one of the benches. I want her away from the water," I ordered.

"What about in the booth?" Heather said.

"Where?" I asked, concentrating more on the oncoming water.

"The booth," she repeated. "It's a good step above the floor of the shelter and there's a small desk in there as well."

"That's a great idea." I turned to face Heather only to see the ticket lady scrambling toward the booth.

"Hey! Wait," I called out. I ran toward her, almost knocking Heather and my daughter to the floor, but it was too late. The woman had the door open and was inside before I could make it to her. The door slammed shut in my face and I heard the click of the lock securing the door. "What are you doing? Open the door."

"There's no room in here for all of us," she said, through the door.

I looked into the small booth and calculated it could at least hold one more adult and a child if put on the small desk. "You can fit another in there and one on the desk. Take my wife and daughter."

"Do you take me for a fool?" she asked. "You don't think I know what you'll do if I open the door. Two adults and a child might squeeze in here, but I'm guessing, if I open the door, I wouldn't be one of those adults, now would I?"

"Don't talk nonsense. Of course, you would. I'm willing to take my chances out here if I can protect my wife and daughter."

"So you say."

"I give you my word."

"Save your breath. I'm not opening up. Besides, read the sign." She pointed a fat finger above her head to a sign attached just above the booth's door. "Employees Only."

"Don't be an idiot. Open up," I screamed at her, as I pounded the door in a rage.

"Get away from the door," she said, as she reached for something under the desk. "If you try to get in here, you'll be sorry." The ticket lady held a sawed-off bat, taped widely around its base.

"You're nuts," I told her, smashing the door with my fist one last time.

"Stop it," Heather called out. "Let her be. You're upsetting Katlyn."

I glared at the woman inside the booth and turned away to join my family.

The water inched its way closer to the three of us so we stepped on top of one of the last benches remaining. The water was only a foot away from us now. After watching the rate some of the other benches had dissolved, I guessed, once the water was finally beneath us, we had about another ten minutes before it too gave way.

"We'll be safe here for a while," I said, keeping a close eye on the rising water. If we had taken the car, would we be in this mess, I wondered? Beating myself up over it wasn't going to help any of us so I tried to push the thought from my mind.

One of the Plexiglass panels cracked from top to bottom. Katlyn screamed at the sudden noise. As the toxic rain continued to beat down on the weakened panel, weblike cracks began to splinter off from the main one.

"Will it hold?" Heather asked, still trying to comfort Katlyn.

"I don't think for much longer, but it's far enough away from us that it shouldn't cause us any immediate problems," I answered.

The temperature increased rapidly in the shelter. My shirt was drenched with sweat.

The cracked panel finally gave way, cascading shards of broken Plexiglass into the shelter. Rain poured in, quickly raising the water level.

"We're going to die," Katlyn cried, burying her face into her Mother's chest.

"No one's going to die, as long as we stay calm," I said. "Others must know what's going on by now and help has to be on its way." I squeezed Katlyn's shoulder but I wasn't sure of our prospects anymore either.

The water already licked at the front legs of the bench we were standing on.

Heather looked at the woman in the booth. "For God's sake, open the door and at least let our daughter in."

The woman didn't respond, instead she looked away.

"You bitch. Have you no heart at all?"

There was still no reply from the woman.

"I hope you die in there," Heather yelled, just as something crashed down onto the roof of the shelter. Everyone jumped. I almost slipped off the bench because of the sudden start. I regained my balance and made sure I was on a more secure footing when I noticed the fine film of moisture on the bench. The heat from the water was making it sweat.

"Watch your footing," I said. "The bench is getting slick." I looked around to see what happened and noticed a large tree branch hanging precariously above the ticket booth. The woman inside noticed it as well and her smug look was gone. I craned my neck to see if there was any damage but couldn't make out anything. "We're all fine, it's just a branch. I don't think there's any damage."

"No, look," Heather said, pointing toward the booth. A thin line of water streamed down the side of one of the booth's windows. The ticket lady in a moment of panic tried to stop the flow with some papers. She screamed out in pain as the water touched her skin. She jerked away in horror, holding her wounded arm and tripped over something, forcing her to crash into the adjacent wall. The booth shuddered from her weight and the stream of water began to come down heavier. The ticket lady got to her feet almost immediately and tried frantically to get the door to the booth open but it seemed stuck.

I carefully moved my way along the bench toward the booth for a better look. I could feel the heat on the bottom of my feet. I took hold of my daughter, picked her up and placed her behind me so I could get by. I maneuvered by my wife next. "Careful," I cautioned her, as I eased by. "And grab hold of Katlyn, the bench is getting slippery."

Almost at the edge of the bench, I saw why the door was stuck. Part of the ceiling where the branch had crashed down was pushed in and wedged against the top frame of the door. I also noticed some buckling of the outside wall. "Stop yanking at the door. I think the door may be the only thing keeping the booth up."

The shelter fell quiet.

"What should we do?" Heather asked. "Can we help her?"

I took another look at the ticket booth and the floor around it. "There's nothing we can do for her. The water has already reached the door. We'd have to step into it to get to her."

Heather didn't respond.

"My feet hurt," Katlyn cried.

"Give her to me," I said, holding out my hands. "I'll carry her on my back for a while." Heather did as I asked and I placed Katlyn on my back in a piggyback position. "How are your feet feeling?" I asked Heather.

"Uncomfortable."

"Can you handle it for a while longer?"

"Do I have a choice?"

I didn't bother to answer. I turned back to the booth and saw the ticket lady standing there as if in shock. "You okay in there?"

The ticket lady turned and looked at me. "I bet you're loving this?" she answered. "The old hag who wouldn't help got what's coming to her. Don't pretend you care if I'm okay or not. If you think that…"

A loud moan floated through the warm sweaty air of the shelter, cutting her off. It was the weight of the branch pushing down on the booth. The outside wall of the booth where it met the door sank a few more inches allowing further trickles of water to seep in.

"Is there nothing we can do?" Heather asked, helplessly. "Maybe we could…"

"I don't want any of your help or your stinking pity," The ticket lady screamed at us from inside her flooding cell. "Take a good look around you. You're in worse shape than me. The waters almost up to the bench now. So save your tears, Honey."

"What's wrong with you? Are you insane?" Heather asked.

The ticket lady started cackling to herself as if she'd just heard the funniest thing in the world.

"Don't worry about her. She must be in shock," I explained.

"That's right Honey. Don't you go worrying about me. I'll be just… Ahhh." The ticket lady screamed out as she whirled around slapping her arms and head. Water streamed from the ceiling of the booth. She pushed herself against the far wall of the booth and nursed her burns, muttering quietly.

"Are we going to die, Daddy?"

"I told you already, no one is going to die," I snapped at my daughter in frustration, making her cry. "I'm sorry, pumpkin. Daddy didn't mean to be cross. It's just that it's so hot in here." But Katlyn didn't buy it and continued sobbing as she buried her face into my shoulder.

Suddenly we heard a loud splash. Was the shelter finally falling apart? The water began to lap onto the top of the bench. We heard another splash and what sounded like engines.

The roar got louder.

The water around us started to ripple and small waves lapped at our feet, melting the soles of our shoes from under us.

Out of the dense rain, two huge vehicles appeared, equipped with spotlights. Beams of light scanned the area as they moved along and Heather and I screamed for help. One of the beams penetrated our disintegrating shelter. The second vehicle panned its spotlight over as well, almost blinding us.

An amplified voice called out, "How many are you?"

"Four," we screamed, over the deafening racket.

"Stay where you are. We're going to get as close as we can."

The large vehicles caused the water to splash up against our legs.

"I don't know if I can stand it anymore," Heather sobbed in pain.

"Just hang in there. We're okay now."

The ticket lady started to slam her body against the door. Which in turn caused more waves in the water.

"Stop it you bitch," Heather screamed.

The water burned into our calves and ankles as one of the vehicles pulled up to the shelter. The voice over the loudspeaker boomed. "We've positioned our side door to the entrance. You'll have to make it to us on your own. Can you do it?"

"I can't do it," Heather said with a sob.

"Of course, you can. It's less than 20 steps."

"You saw what happened to the others. I just don't think that…"

A sudden gush of steaming hot air blasted our faces and the shelter around us shuddered. A horrific crash brought our attention back toward the ticket booth. Part of the ceiling had given way and water flooded quickly into the booth. The ticket lady screamed in pain and threw herself against the walls frantically. The water was already up to her hips and then quickly to her midriff.

"Turn Katlyn away," Heather ordered.

I managed to turn Katlyn away just in time.

The water lifted the ticket woman's thrashing body and pressed it against the window directly behind us. The ticket lady's clothes burned away as her flesh bubbled red as a lobster in boiling water.

She went under a few times, reappearing each time with less and less hair until she was finally bald and her scalp racked with blisters. Eventually, the water reached the ceiling and the ticket lady became completely submerged and melted away before our eyes. The water then started to spill over-the-top of the booth and into the shelter.

"We have to do it now," I said.

"You go first and take Katlyn."

"No, we go together."

"I'm so scared." Heather cried uncontrollably.

"Take Katlyn," I told her.

"No, I can't."

"Take her," I said again, taking Katlyn from my back and handing her to Heather.

"No Robert, please don't do this."

"Just take her and put her on your back." I pushed Katlyn onto her and Katlyn instinctively grabbed for her Mother and wouldn't let go. Heather gave in and helped Katlyn into position. I took a deep breath and stepped into the churning water and gritted my teeth as a hiss of pain escaped from between my clenched lips.

"Climb onto my back and for God's sake hold tight to Katlyn." The pain was almost unbearable and I wondered if I was going to be able to pull this off. I felt the sudden extra weight of my wife and daughter as they climbed onto me. "Hurry, I don't know how much longer I can last." I looked quickly toward the booth. The ticket lady floated eerily in the bloody water.

The water seemed to be alive around her as if filled with piranha's, quickly devouring their prey.

With my wife and daughter clinging desperately to me I stumbled my way to the waiting vehicle and safety. With each step, I felt bits of my feet dissolve away. I didn't look down for fear of what I might find. With only a few steps left I was almost sure I had nothing left but stumps, but I somehow forced myself on.

I made out the opening in the vehicle and pushed myself forward. I carefully turned myself around and a pair of hands from within the vehicle appeared and grabbed Katlyn and pulled her in. What seemed to be almost an eternity of pain ended with Heather being dragged to safety as well. I felt myself begin to collapse from exhaustion and pain into the deadly water but it didn't matter now that my family was safe. As I felt myself start to drift into unconsciousness a pair of hands grabbed me and dragged me into the safety of the vehicle.

The trapdoor to the vehicle slammed shut. The mechanized machine slowly pulled away as the entire shelter collapsed into nothing but food for the churning water. The ticket lady, now nothing more than a flowing ebb of blood and small bits of flesh, disappeared into the bubbling, destructive force of nature.

Although I didn't know it yet, I'd never walk again without artificial support but at least my family and I were alive and I would live out my days knowing I was a hero in my daughter's eyes.

What more could a father ask for.

ORPHANS

"I'm going upstairs to poke my eyes out," Sandra told her parents as she got up from the kitchen table. Her parents looked at one another, and after a moment, smiled and excused her from the table.

Ever since the change, Sandra, who everyone called Sam for short, liked to say absurd things to confuse them. She realized they weren't her parents anymore. Not since the freak lightning storm a week ago.

The television came on in the living room as Sam walked up the stairs to check on her brother, Billy. As she climbed upstairs, she heard the usual high-pitched wail coming from the TV. The sound sent shivers through her. As curious as she was, she'd never been able to see what her parents watched since they only turned on the TV when they were alone.

Once, she'd rushed into the room but by the time she'd arrived the wails had stopped and the television was already turned off.

Upstairs there were three bedrooms and two bathrooms. Sam and Billy shared one of the bathrooms, the other was an ensuite attached to their parent's bedroom. A few days ago, their dad put a lock on it. Needless to say, Sam was very interested to know what was in there.

Billy's bedroom was the first door on the right, at the top of the stairs. Presently, the door was closed. Sam used their secret knock. "It's open," her brother said. Sam opened the door and walked in, shutting the door behind her.

The room's walls were plastered with sports posters. Soccer, hockey, baseball and football stars covered every inch of wall space. The only poster not sports-oriented was a creepy looking poster of a giant crow he had right above his bed. Sam had no idea where Billy had got it from or why he even had it. He had a desk in one corner with a bookcase beside it and a long bureau with a mirror attached to it along the adjacent wall. Billy's bed, where he currently sat, was against the far wall by the window.

"How are you doing?" Sam asked.

Billy looked up from his portable video game player. "What do you think?"

Sam sat down beside him and noticed the dried streaks of tears on his cheeks. She leaned back against the headboard and brought her hands up behind her head. "Think they know what we're up to?" she asked.

"Don't know."

Sam was older than Billy by only two years but that was ages in kid's years. They were close enough but had never been buddies. The freak lightning storm had brought them closer together once they realized all they had in the world were each other now.

"Are you ready for tonight?" Sam asked.

Billy turned to look at her. "Yes."

"What if we're wrong?"

"We're not."

Sam sat up and picked at a few loose threads on Billy's comforter. "How do you know?"

Billy rolled his eyes. "They tried to kill me tonight, remember?"

"Maybe it was just a mistake." Billy had a peanut allergy, so when their mom brought in peanut butter cookies for dessert, Billy and Sam couldn't believe it.

Billy snorted. "Yeah right. The woman who inspected every piece of food I've ever eaten mistakenly serves me the one thing that's sure to kill me?"

They fell silent.

"Did you set the clock?" Sam finally asked.

"Yes," he answered, not bothering to look up from his game.

"For what time?"

Billy slid over on the bed and pressed a button on his alarm clock. The clock sat on a small side table beside his bed. When he pressed the button, the clock showed that the alarm was set for midnight.

"Do you have the stuff?" Sam asked.

Billy hopped off the bed and reached under it, bringing out two axes.

Sam felt light-headed. She wasn't sure if she had the strength to go through with it. She could see the resolve in Billy's face though. He was ready and raring to go.

The only comfort Sam felt was in the fact they weren't alone in this. It wasn't just their parents, it was everyone else's as well. Sure, she'd noticed that after the strange lightning storm her parents began acting odd. But it wasn't until Jarred started rallying the other kids in the schoolyard that things began to fall into place.

Jarred was a bit older than the rest of the kids so he knew things the others didn't. He was also a big horror fan. He'd watched all the good horror movies and read all the best horror books. Everything Sam's parents had never allowed in the house. So he knew how to read all the signs and convinced all the kids to watch for strange activities. The bizarre storm, the sudden change in the way their parents acted, the same strange television channel all their parents watched.

It wasn't until all the parents added locks to their bathroom doors that Sam finally believed it all. Tonight though had been the final straw after she watched in horror as her mother brought in the peanut butter cookies.

Still, could she do what had to be done?

"I think I'll stay in here with you tonight," Sam said.

Billy didn't answer. He stood and stared at the gleam from the axe blade he held in his hands.

"Do you remember what Jarred said to do?" Sam asked.

Billy put the axe down. "I got it." He pushed the two axes under his bed and out of sight. "How far do you think this thing has spread?"

"I don't know," she said. "As far as the storm covered, I guess."

"You think other kids are doing this?"

Sam frowned as she looked at her brother. "I don't know that either."

Billy hopped back on the bed and grabbed his video game player. He turned it off and put it on his side table. "You know Tom Sable?"

"Yeah, you know I do, why?" Sam was surprised by this change in topic.

Billy grinned. "He likes you."

"Shut up."

"I'm serious. Alex told me."

Sam punched Billy in the arm. "Then Alex is a liar."

"That's what I thought but I spoke with Tom afterward and it's true."

Sam felt herself blush. "Why'd you do that?"

"I figured with everything going on you might want to hear some good news."

Sam moved in for another punch but Billy moved too quickly. "What makes you think that would be good news anyway, you loser?" She asked.

"Because I heard you tell Brittany that you thought he was cute."

Sam threw herself at her brother and the two of them toppled off the bed with a crash.

"You were listening in on my telephone calls."

Billy pushed her off with his feet and Sam staggered back. She was about to say something when the bedroom door flew open.

"What's going on in here?" their father demanded.

At first, Sam thought their real father was back. That was just how he would have acted and she felt a creeping uncertainty cloud her mind.

"We were having sex," Billy said.

Sam stood with her mouth open unable to utter a sound.

"Fine then," their father said. "Just keep it down."

"Sure thing," Billy said with a half salute.

Their dad closed the door. If Sam ever had a doubt in her mind it was gone now.

"You're a pig," she said.

"I just wanted to make sure it wasn't really Dad."

"I think you made your point."

They slumped down on the bed. Sam thought about Tom and felt a tightening in her stomach. Could it be possible he really liked her? He was an only child so maybe she could convince him to hook up with Billy and her after everything was done.

She turned to ask Billy a question but he'd fallen asleep. She wasn't surprised. They hadn't slept in days, too busy preparing for tonight. She stared at her brother and wondered if any of the other kids were as nervous as she was. After tonight though, that would all be over.

Sam noticed a framed picture lying face down on the dresser. She got off the bed, walked over to it and picked it up. It was a picture of their family up at the cottage they'd rented last summer.

That had been a great summer. She and Billy had spent most of it on the beach or in the water. It had also been the summer she'd first met Tom. He was funny and so cute. She felt that tightening in her stomach again and smiled. She put the picture down and looked at herself in the mirror. She turned slowly to the side and breathed in a deep breath hoping to accentuate her breasts. It didn't work.

As she thought back, she remembered the local ice cream parlor they'd walk to each night after dinner. Billy always ordered the butterscotch sundae while she ordered a strawberry ice cream cone. Mom ate nothing but chocolate ice cream and Dad always had an orange popsicle. Boring and predictable, but what she wouldn't do to have her good old boring family back.

She turned away from the mirror and climbed back into bed with her brother. She watched the slow up and down movements of his chest as he slept. The rhythmic movements relaxed her and for the first time in days, she fell asleep.

The alarm went off at midnight. Sam turned lazily to her brother and saw his eyes were wide open and staring at the ceiling. She rolled over on her back and stared up at the ceiling as well.

Billy climbed out of bed and walked to the door. He placed an ear to it and listened.

"Hear anything?" Sam asked.

Billy shook his head and placed his ear back to the door.

Sam sat up. Her stomach was in knots but it wasn't the good kind of knots she got from thinking about Tom. These were different. As she watched her brother listening at the door, she brought her knees up to her chin and waited.

Billy turned off his bedroom light and slowly opened the door. The hallway was almost as dark as their parents' bedroom, the only light coming from the nightlight in the bathroom. He left the door open for a few minutes, listening for anything that would alert them that their parents were awake.

There wasn't a sound.

Sam watched Billy walk through the door to the top of the staircase. He looked down the stairs and immediately came back, shutting the door behind him.

The lights came on and Sam blinked away the harsh glare. "Well?" she asked.

"They're asleep," he said.

She jumped off the bed and reached under it for the axes. She brought them out and cradled them against her chest as she sat back down on the bed. She could feel the tears filling up in the corner of her eyes. The whole thing was crazy. How were they supposed to live without their parents to support them? What if they were wrong and they got arrested? Or worse, what if they were right and didn't do anything until it was too late? Tears ran freely down her face.

After a few deep breaths, Sam loosened her hold on the axes and set them down on the bed. "Are we doing the right thing?" she asked.

"You know we are."

"I don't know if I can do it."

Billy picked up one of the axes. "I can do it myself if you want."

She stared at him. How could he be so cool about it? She knew she couldn't let him do it alone. That would be unfair. Plus, Jarred made it quite clear that to be in the group you had to be a participant. If you weren't in on the kill then you weren't in the group. Simple as that.

Sam wiped away her tears and picked up the remaining axe.

They walked slowly out of the bedroom, their footsteps muffled by the rug. The night light in the bathroom cast a sickly yellow glow across the wall. Her heartbeat quickened with every step and once again she doubted if she could go through with their plan.

Billy was nothing more than a blur in front of her and she wished he'd slow down. She had a sudden urge to discuss the whole situation again with him. She looked down at the blade of the axe she held and it seemed to wink at her in the yellow glow. She looked up to find Billy but he had already disappeared into the darkness of their parents' bedroom.

She stopped and took a few deep breaths and tried to think about what Jarred had told them. One quick chop across the neck was all it would take he had assured them. Even if the head didn't come right off, he guaranteed their parents would be as good as dead and that they should leave the room immediately and head towards the rendezvous point.

A cold sweat broke out across Sam's forehead as she forced her legs forward. Before she knew it, she was standing on the opposite side of the bed from Billy, looking down at their sleeping parents.

There was no turning back now.

She watched as Billy raised his axe over their mother. As Sam raised her axe, she thought back on all the good times their family had shared and she suddenly realized she didn't care what Jarred said. She lowered her axe and shook her head in the darkness.

Billy didn't hesitate. He slammed the axe down on his mother's neck and yanked it back with incredible speed. With a cry that reminded Sam of the war cries she'd heard coming from the Indians in the old westerns, she watched her brother jump onto the bed, bringing down the axe several times on their father. She felt a wave of nausea wash through her like a tsunami. She threw her hands to her mouth and ran for the door.

The door slammed shut before she reached it. The room went pitch black as Sam stopped and let out a short scream.

"Billy?" she said.

There was no response.

"Billy, where are you?"

Sam trembled, unsure what exactly was going on. "I don't think this is funny."

A scratch sounded behind her and the smell of sulfur filled the air. Sam was too afraid to turn around as she squeezed her eyes shut. As she stood trembling, she thought she heard something dripping. In her imagination she pictured her parents' blood dripping to the floor from the bed like wax from a candle. She finally broke down in sobs, unable to take it anymore. She slowly turned around and opened her eyes.

Sam's eyes widened when she saw the reason for her brother's silence. Billy hung like a broken puppet at the end of her fathers' arm. Blood dripped from the massive gash across Billy's neck. In her father's other hand was a single candle.

"I'm sorry," she whispered as the tears streaked down her face.

An ugly sneer appeared across her father's face. "Too late for sorry," he said. He parted his lips and flickering, short tendrils shot from his mouth as if to taste the air around them. A high-pitched wail, the same wail which came from that mysterious channel on their television set, emanated from the twisting tendrils until she thought it was going to drive her mad.

She turned away and noticed the stuffed pillowcases hanging half off the bed.

They'd been tricked.

Sam turned back to her father, ready to plead for her life when a cold hand clutched her shoulder. She jumped away from its grasp and turned to see her mother standing behind her, holding one of the axes.

As the axe came down, Sam wondered if Tom really liked her.

A LATE NIGHT CALL

JUNE 1998

The phone rang, waking Frank in the middle of the night.

"Hello?" he muttered, still half asleep.

"Help me," a faint women's voice pleaded. The line went dead.

"Hello? Hello?" Frank gripped the receiver, wide awake now. The voice spooked him with its eerie cry for help. The buzzing sound of a disconnected line sent a shiver down his spine.

He hated late night calls. It was always bad news. He wanted to press the code and see what number had called, but he couldn't remember how to do it.

The voice seemed familiar though.

Frank hung up the receiver, stretched out under his blankets and stared up at the dark ceiling. The room was pitch-black and he couldn't make out a thing, but he had a strange feeling he wasn't alone. He held his breath and listened.

Nothing.

He continued to lie there but with his imagination racing, he had to check it out. He slowly drew his arm out from under the covers and inched it towards the bedside lamp. He felt the base of the lamp and reached up, trying to find the switch. Finally, his fingers came across the switch.

He pressed it.

Nothing. He pressed it again but still no light came on.

He didn't move a muscle but listened carefully for any telltale clue he might not be alone. The only sound though came from his heart racing inside his chest. Then he remembered. He'd unplugged the light to plug in the vacuum earlier and must have forgotten to plug it back in.

He continued to lie in his bed, frustration building with every second that passed.

He bolted from the bed and dashed over to the wall to the light switch. He found it, flipped the switch and a wash of light lit up the room.

A sense of relief came over him when he saw he was alone.

The phone rang.

He jumped at the sudden noise but managed to pull himself together once he realized it was only the phone. He walked slowly to the phone as if it might be able to bite him and stared at the receiver. It rang again and he picked it up.

"Hello?"

This time there was just crackling on the line. He could hear sounds somewhere in the background but couldn't make them out.

"Hello?" he said again, only to be answered by more crackling on the line.

He put down the phone and looked nervously around the room. He went to the bedroom door, peeked out into the hallway and then walked slowly to his closet and looked inside. All clear. He felt silly and was glad no one was around to see his childish antics. After one more look around, he flicked the light off and hopped back into bed.

The phone rang again.

Frank grabbed for the phone in the dark almost ripping the cord from the wall.

"What?"

Nothing but more crackling.

Fed up, Frank was about to slam the receiver down when through the crackling, he thought he heard a woman crying.

"Hello? Is anybody there?" he asked.

More static, then, "Dear God, can anybody hear me? Please help me. I'm alone and I can hear it coming."

The phone went dead.

Frank sprang from his bed and hit the light switch as he stormed by it. His toes dug into the rug, muffling the sound of his footsteps as he made his way down the hallway. He flew down the stairs, turned on the hall light and yanked open the drawer of the hall table that held the phone.

He found what he was looking for and carried the ancient phone book to the couch. He threw himself on it and began rifling through the pages. Then he found it, *69, the code to find out the phone number of the last caller. He walked back to the phone with a grin of accomplishment, picked up the receiver and pressed the code. After the message ended, the grin faded from his face. It seemed the last caller was him. He remembered the call vividly, made from his office earlier in the day. He'd called to remind himself that his dry cleaning would be ready for pick up the next day. Why hadn't the last call come up, he wondered as he climbed the stairs? He'd just made it back to the bedroom when the phone began to ring again. He raced to the phone and snatched the receiver from its cradle.

"Who are you?"

More crackling filtered down the line.

"Who is this? What kind of game are you playing?"

Breathing heavier after his verbal assault on the phone, he listened, but nothing more than crackling could be heard. Had he surprised the caller with his aggressiveness? He hoped so. Maybe it would be enough to get them to stop calling. Then the same faint female voice drifted through the crackling.

"Is anybody there? Please help me. If anyone can hear me, please do something. I'm trapped here and I can hear it coming. I am at AU1-5555. My address is. . ."

The phone went dead.

Frank couldn't move. That voice. It was so haunting. It had to be some childish prank, yet he couldn't get over how sincere the voice sounded. Whoever she was, she was good at this game. Good enough to have given him a real fright. He finally realized he was still holding the phone when it began beeping at him. He hung up immediately, then picked up the line again and pressed 0.

"Operator, may I assist you?"

"Yes, I'm hoping you can. I've been getting crank calls this evening that I can't trace by pressing *69 and I wondered if you could help me?"

"What is the nature of the call sir?"

"Uh, it's a woman pleading for help. She says something's coming, but I'm sure it's a prank."

"Have you notified the authorities?"

"No, I just called you because I'd like to know where the calls are coming from."

"One minute please."

Frank waited as a barrage of the company's products and services played on endlessly. He looked around the room absentmindedly and again began to feel he wasn't alone again.

"Hello, sir?"

"Yes, I'm still here."

"We have recorded no calls coming to your home phone number this evening."

"The woman on the phone told me her number was AU1-5555. I'm sure it's a false number but maybe that will help."

"I think someone is trying to pull your leg sir."

"Yes, I realize that but what am I supposed to do?'

"No sir, I mean that phone number no longer exists. It was an old exchange that is no longer in use."

"What do you mean?"

"Those numbers were used for party lines and haven't been in existence for over fifty years."

"Is there any other way I can track down where the calls came from?"

"I suggest if the calls persist, you call the authorities. Perhaps they can tap your line for you. Is there anything else I can help you with this evening, sir?"

"No, thanks anyway."

He hung up the phone no further ahead than he'd been when he'd started. He reached down, found the bedside lamp's plug and placed it back into the socket. The glow of the single light lit up the room but created many new shadows that added to the creepiness of the entire incident. He thanked God he wouldn't have to get up for work in the morning as he didn't work Mondays. He looked over at the phone as if expecting it to ring again but decided he'd had enough for the evening and took it off the hook.

The next day he found himself raring to go. It was as if during his brief sleep he had subconsciously come up with a plan.

After getting dressed and grabbing a quick bite to eat, he was out the door and headed to the public library. Once there he put his plan into effect.

Frank went through index after index of microfiche until he eventually found what he was looking for. The last known subscriber to AU1-5555 was a Harold Bretton of 93 Oak Street in Aultsville. That city rang a bell but he couldn't figure out from where. He was sure it was within driving distance of his home though.

Aultsville, it turned out, after he checked out a map, was only an hour's drive down the highway, along the banks of the St. Lawrence Seaway that connected the American and Canadian borders. As the next day was July 1st and he didn't have to work, he decided he would drive to Aultsville and check it out. Luckily his sleep that night was uninterrupted. The sun was shining and it was a perfect day for a drive so he didn't waste time getting underway. He made it to the Seaway in no time and began snaking his way through the small villages looking for Aultsville. He eventually spotted a sign pointing away from the road and toward the waterfront. He turned onto the road and followed it for a while until it became a dirt road. He continued down the bumpy dirt road until it ended abruptly with two metal posts blocking the way.

He sat in his car wondering what he should do. His curiosity finally got the better of him and he parked the car and got out to have a look around.

He didn't see a town, only forest as far as the eye could see. Just after the posts, a small dirt walking path led to the waterfront. He decided to follow it. Water began to creep up on both sides of him as the forest receded into the background. He looked around but there wasn't a soul in sight.

Then why did he have the feeling he wasn't alone?

After walking for a bit the shoreline came into view. Shaped like a cove, the shoreline meandered away in the distance. There was still no town he could see, nor any people for that matter.

He gazed across the water and took in his surroundings. Broken rocks and strange boulders littered the shoreline. The trees he passed all appeared to be either dead or dying. He felt like he was in a graveyard.

"Help me," a women's voice suddenly called out, sending a chill through his body.

Frank looked around but didn't see anybody.

"Help me," the voice begged again. He recognized it as the same voice that had called the other night. As he walked along the shoreline something deep in the water caught his eye.

It was a light. Or at least he thought it was a light. He stopped in his tracks and turned toward where he thought he'd seen it and watched carefully. From somewhere in the depths of the water a single light blinked on and off. He felt a coldness run through him like he'd never experienced before. He slowly backed away from the water's edge. He felt like if he got too close to the water something might reach out and grab him, pulling him down into the depths toward the mysterious light. He sidestepped along the shoreline giving himself a wide berth from the water's edge but continued looking out into it.

Again, from somewhere below the waterline, a light flashed on and off. Could someone be trapped down there? A diver perhaps? Where the hell was the town? He needed to find somebody to help him because the place was giving him the creeps. He yelled out for help. There was nothing but silence, yet the light continued to blink its lonely signal from the deep.

Frank had had enough. He needed to get out of there and find help. He ran along the waterfront and got back onto the path that led to his car. When he arrived at the metal posts, he knew he had a problem.

The car was gone.

He ran around looking for his car but had no luck. He sat in a gully on the side of the road and waited in vain for someone to drive by. After a half-hour of waiting for a passing motorist, he decided it wasn't going to happen. He resigned himself to the fact he'd have to make his way back to the highway on foot, so he started walking.

As it became darker, he scolded himself for not having set out earlier. He was walking along the gloomy dirt road toward the highway when he suddenly heard rustling in the bushes just to his left. He picked up his pace but so did the rustling. What kind of a nightmare had he gotten himself into? He began to sprint down the road when the rustling turned into a thunderous roar. It sounded like the trees were crashing all around him. In a panic he tripped, falling to the ground hard. If he was hurt, he didn't know it or didn't care because he was up and running again. He thought he was gaining some ground when a thunderous crash rang out from just ahead. He barely had enough time to stop before a huge tree crashed down in front of him. Lying on the ground panting, Frank thought he might start to cry.

He was alone in some Godforsaken forest with something he couldn't see hunting him down and night coming on quick. He continued lying there until he couldn't hear anything moving anymore. He looked around and everything seemed back to normal or as normal as things could be out here in the middle of nowhere. He got up, brushed himself off and examined the mess in front of him that now blocked the road. After examining it he decided he didn't want to try climbing over it, especially with no one around to help him out if he got hurt. High above him circled a murder of crows and Frank wondered if they knew something he didn't.

He turned around and made his way back to where the car had been. There was no more rustling or crashing in the forest, only complete silence. As night approached so did the bugs and they were ferocious. After a dozen bites, he decided he'd be drained of blood by morning if he stayed put, so he headed back to the waterfront. He hoped by the water the bugs wouldn't be as bad, but not being an outdoorsman, he had no idea what to expect.

On arrival back at the waterfront, the blinking light in the water greeted him. From where he stood, he couldn't see much, but as he peered into the water, he could make out shapes underneath the murky water. He looked around for a better vantage point and found what he was looking for. Just down the shoreline was a tall clump of rocks. He carefully climbed to the top, sat down and searched the water for the light. There it was, going on and off like a camera flash.

He must be hallucinating because what he saw looked like an entire town under the water.

Aultsville?

He waited patiently on top of his perch for the next flash of light. When it lit up again Frank strained to take it all in. Sure enough, there beneath the water were different types of buildings. He continued his vigil well into the night until finally fatigue overcame him and he fell into a deep sleep.

"Help me, Frank," a scared voice called out.

"What do you want from me?" he answered back.

"I'm alone and so afraid. I can hear it coming. Please do something."

"Hear what? What can I do?"

"Come get me, Frank. Save me," she begged, crying.

Frank found himself on a hill looking down at the homes below. There was a sign. It read, Aultsville, in small black letters. Although he didn't know what was happening, he knew this was a dream. A dream he wanted to wake up from but couldn't.

"Help me. You're so close. Can you hear it coming?"

"I don't know where you are and I can't hear anything. What are you doing to me?"

"You have to help me, Frank, you're my only hope. Hurry, it's coming."

"What's coming? Stop talking in riddles. What do you want from me?" he cried out in frustration.

"Follow the light," she answered.

Like in most dreams everything moved in slow motion. He seemed headed towards town but never got any closer no matter how much he walked.

Then he saw the light.

From an upstairs room of a house, it blinked on and off, on and off. He was able to make out the street name at the corner closest to the house. Oak Street, the same street he had looked up earlier at the library. He continued his fruitless walk toward town, but although he appeared to be getting no closer, with each step taken he was able to see things more clearly. He could see a form in the window now, like a shadow, illuminated by the light.

Was it her?

A deafening sound filled the air. A similar noise to what he had heard following him in the forest earlier. What was it? It seemed much more intense now, Frank became scared.

"Hurry Frank, it's almost here. Help me, before it's too late."

His legs felt like they were running through deep mud. He frantically tried to get free and felt panic begin to stretch his nerves. Should he try to run away? He knew he couldn't. He had to help this woman, whatever the cost, but he didn't know why.

He edged down the hill as best he could, his legs straining against whatever force was slowing them down.

As the horrible sound grew closer, panic set in with earnest. He reached the bottom of the hill and found himself on street level. After fighting with his legs to get down the hill he had managed to lose sight of the house. He frantically looked around trying to get his bearings but it was hard to concentrate with the sound of roaring thunder in his ears. He yelled out to the mysterious voice.

"Where are you? Call out to me so I can find you."

If she was calling out to him, he couldn't make it out over the horrific noise. He ran down the vacant streets. Where was everybody? Didn't they hear the thunderous maelstrom heading their way? Street after street he searched, turning one corner after another, almost deafened by the sounds around him and finally, he spotted it. At the top of the street, a house with a light on its upper floor blinking on and off like an SOS.

He had found it, or was it too late?

The next thing he knew he was at the house, but how had he got there? It didn't matter. He ran to the front door, burst into the house and called out to her. He made his way through the house but could hear nothing but the roar which seemed all around him. He tried to wake himself again from this nightmare but couldn't. He charged up the stairs to the deafening sounds of explosions and snapping wood.

Disoriented, he wasn't sure which way to go. All the doors were shut and the racket around him prevented him from hearing her cries. Door after door he swung open to nothing. He finally found the room, but to his horror, he was too late.

Tied to a chair her lifeless body stared at him accusingly. She had been stabbed to death, the murder weapon lay by her feet, covered in blood. Once again panic coursed through his body, his mind started to come apart. He staggered through the room like a drunken man, crying into his hands, all sense of rationality leaving him. He was going mad. The sound of a thunderclap broke him momentarily from of his trance and he staggered to the window overlooking the town below.

He gazed out the window and his blood stopped. A wall of water, higher than he could have ever imagined tore through the town, headed straight toward him like a freight train, snapping buildings and homes into tinder. It ripped a path of destruction directly toward him. He had just enough time to let out a scream before the single light blinked off for the last time.

"Thank you," a women's faint voice called out.

The next day, three fishermen found what they thought was a man sleeping on top of a cluster of rocks. On closer inspection, they found they'd been wrong. Soaking wet and his mouth filled with water, the man was dead.

The fishermen scanned the shoreline for others who may have met the same fate but all they found was the back end of a car sticking out of the water.

The next day the local newspaper ran this story.

After an exhaustive search by the police diving team, the re-mains of Marie Bretton were found tied to a chair in the room of what was once her Aultsville home. Authorities believe her now-deceased husband, Harold Bretton was responsible and are labeling it a murder.

There has always been speculation that many townspeople rid themselves of their dirty laundry when the Americans and Canadi-ans agreed to open the St. Lawrence Seaway for larger boat traffic. The notice had been given that on July 1st, 1958, Aultsville, as well as a few other towns along the Seaway, would soon be underwater after the opening of the dam upriver. All residents were helped, if needed, to relocate possessions out of the area. Although much was moved, just as many things stayed behind to face the torrents of water that would soon engulf this sleepy village.

At this time there is no explanation how Frank Mason or his car managed to end up where they did. Locals however speak of a rumor concerning the missing Bretton child who disappeared one winter's day. Many speculated that Marie spirited the child away to another family because of Harold's abusive temper. Locals who are familiar with the family remark how the dead body of Frank Mason had a remarkable likeness to Harold himself. Others just chalk it up to another mystery of the 'Lost Villages of the Seaway.'

Author's Note

Although this is a fictional story, Aultsville was a real place that consisted of close to 400 people, one of them a relative of mine. On July 1st, 1958, the St. Lawrence Seaway was opened to allow larger ship traffic to enter the interior and with it, the Village of Aultsville and a few other towns nearby disappeared forever. They now all lie beneath the water holding whatever mysteries they contain, safe from prying eyes.

HARMONY

CHAPTER ONE

Somehow, it managed to get around me. I couldn't see it, but I could sense its presence. I crouched low against a tree and waited.

The day had started like any other, grading papers of the recruits the military saw fit to send me. It was tedious work but I managed to plod through it. I graded the last paper, put them into a folder and tidied my desk. I left my tiny basement office with its industrial painted walls and cold concrete floors and, hoping to clear my head, set off on my run.

I crossed the base and ran towards the lake. The spring air felt chilly but the last of the snow had disappeared a few days before. I followed the shore of the lake, the early morning sun glimmering across its calm waters until I came to the forest that surrounded the perimeter of the military base.

The path I followed squished under my feet from the melted snow. I continued on the muddy path, taking in the scents of the awakening forest after its long winter sleep. My cell phone rang as I reached the halfway point of my daily run.

"Cross here," I answered.

"Where are you?" a gruff voice barked. I recognized it immediately as General Ryan, my commanding officer.

"West perimeter, halfway through my run, sir."

There was a brief pause. "I'm sending a jeep. Rendezvous with it by the firing range." The line went dead.

I left the path and cut through the forest, hopping over stumps and dodging trees along the way. I broke from the forest and found

I'd guessed right. The firing range, where I trained men on the fine art of marksmanship, was dead ahead. The jeep was already waiting.

My two companions said nothing on the drive back. I used the time to stare at my shoes and socks which were both soaked and muddy from the numerous puddles I'd splashed through. I expected them to take me straight to General Ryan's office but it surprised me to see us headed towards Hangar 12 instead. As we approached, the General appeared through its front doors.

We pulled up to the hangar and I got out and walked toward Ryan as the jeep drove away. "Good morning, General," I said with a smile.

"Nothing good about it," he remarked. "Follow me into the hangar." Ryan had his hair cropped short. He stood over six feet tall and had the frame of a tank.

I followed him and he led me to a table with some charts and maps on it. Waiting for him to say whatever he had on his mind I glanced at the papers on the table.

"Recognize anything?" he asked.

"Yes, it's Fort Harmony."

"Very good, considering you're a civilian and Harmony is one of the military's best-kept secrets."

I didn't respond. The door to the hangar opened and I turned.

"James Cross, this is a surprise," the new arrival commented.

"Major Warrant," I acknowledged.

Warrant walked to the table where Ryan and I stood and looked down at the papers. "Hell's Gate?"

"You will not refer to Fort Harmony by that name again, understood Major?"

"Yes General."

Ryan shuffled through the papers on the table and seemed to be trying to organize them into a specific order. I waited patiently, not saying a word. I studied Warrant, wondering why he was here and if he knew any more than I did. It was odd to have the two of us in one room together and I didn't like it. Although in my military days I had never reached a rank higher than Sergeant, in the field, we were equals.

"Gentlemen, we have a situation," the General said. "There's been an incident at Fort Harmony and it's a class A fuck up."

"And we're here to clean it up?" Warrant asked.

"Correct," the General said.

I knew little of Fort Harmony or as Warrant referred to it, Hell's Gate. I did know it was a top-secret research and development base with the highest security but that was about it. Everything else I'd heard were either rumors or speculation. The rumors ran the gamut between biological weapons to secret alien technology. "What's our role in all this?" I asked.

"Simple, we need the two of you to eliminate anything and everything you deem a threat within your areas of operation."

"That's a pretty open agenda," I commented.

"Yes, it is and any act of termination is purely at your discretion."

"So Cross and I aren't working together as a team then?" Warrant asked.

The General seemed to choose his words carefully. "You will be working in two separate fields of operation but as a team. Either of you can request support from the other but we would prefer that doesn't happen. We need to cover as much ground as possible, as quickly as possible, understood?"

I nodded. "How many potential targets are there?"

"Unknown at this time but our best intelligence at the moment tells us we have half a dozen liabilities on the move."

"Do we have descriptions or pictures?" Warrant asked.

"No."

I got the feeling this assignment might get messy. "How will we know who's a friendly and who isn't?"

The General stepped closer to the table and motioned for us to do the same. "These are your fields of operation," he said, pointing at the map showing Fort Harmony and its surrounding areas. "Major, you'll cover the south and west quadrants. Cross, the north and east. You can consider anything you meet within your fields of operation as hostile."

"Anything?" I asked.

"Anything. You have total discretion on this one. Eliminate anything you come across. I wish I could tell you more but this is a sensitive project and it's on a need-to-know basis only." The General pulled a larger map from the bottom of the pile and flattened it out on the table. "What I can tell you is that there's a five-mile perimeter around the base currently patrolled by Special Forces with orders of shoot to kill. Anything within the five-mile perimeter is a free-fire zone so watch yourselves."

Warrant looked at me but there was no trace of his usual cocky smile. His brown eyes studied me and I guessed he was wondering how much I knew. He wasn't as tall as Ryan but taller than me and leaner.

Whatever had happened was big. Bigger than any operation I'd ever participated in. I looked away and stared at the gray walls of the hangar as if they might reveal some answers but they didn't.

"Sir," Warrant broke the silence.

"Yes?"

"I beg your pardon, but we've all heard the rumors that float around about the base and I'd like to know a bit more about what we're up against."

"All we know is we have up to half a dozen hostile targets within this area," he answered, pointing at the map of Fort Harmony. "With information vital to the security of this nation, they cannot escape our perimeter alive. Now, gentlemen, time is of the essence. I need you to suit up and prepare your gear because we move out in thirty minutes."

"That's not enough time to pull my gear together and get back here," I said, surprised at the time frame. "I need more time than that. I still have to call my son to let him know I'll be away for a bit."

The General seemed uneasy and I guessed what he was about to say. "I'm sorry, there'll be no calls until after the mission. We can't take any risks. All your gear is here already, over there in the locker room." The General pointed towards the far wall.

The locker room stank of sweat and I wondered when they'd last hosed it down.

Warrant searched through his gear as he mumbled something to himself. I recognized my stuff spread out on a bench in the far corner and walked over to it. I picked up my rifle first and checked it out. All my scopes were there and everything seemed to be in order. Just to be sure, I broke my rifle down and put it back together.

"How's your gear?" Warrant called out from across the room.

"Looks like they cleaned and greased it for me. You?"

"Same. We must be special." The two of us laughed.

I stuffed some of my camouflage gear into my bag. "So, what do you make of all this?"

"I don't like it."

"Me either," I said. "What do you know about Harmony?"

Warrant had his rifle lifted against his shoulder as he checked out his scopes. "Probably no more than you do."

"That's not very helpful."

He put his rifle down and grinned at me. "I don't think they're telling us everything if that's what you want to know."

"Oh, you can bet on that."

As he began to break down his rifle he said, "I've heard all sorts of crazy things about the place. My guess is they work on biological warfare crap."

"You think they had a breach of security and someone found a buyer for whatever the hell they produce up there?"

Warrant began separating his ammo. "I think they had an accident and some of the wackos that work there left the base before they could quarantine it."

"No, they would've told us if we were dealing with a contagion."

"Why?"

"I don't know," I said, "I just think they would have."

Warrant smiled. "You should have stayed in the corps, the way you believe everything they dish out."

"I would have. It was their choice, not mine."

"That's right, I heard something about that. You wouldn't complete a mission."

"I don't want to talk about it." I continued to stuff my gear into my bag.

"It was because of a child, wasn't it?" Warrant put down his gear and walked up to where I was packing my stuff.

"You know exactly why, so I don't see any reason for this conversation."

He sat down on the bench beside me. "It is important because I need to know I can count on you out there."

"You know you can."

"Do I?"

I sighed. "My target had a child in the car and I knew if I terminated him, there was a chance the child might die in the ensuing crash, so I aborted. Happy?"

He said nothing. I didn't know if my answer was what he'd been hoping to hear but I didn't care. In the same situation, I would do it again. I continued packing.

"Tough call," he said. Without another word he got up and went back to his packing.

The General entered the room with a cough. Warrant and I stood up. He wasn't alone. "Warrant, Cross, this is Doctor Meredith Slaughter."

We both nodded.

"Doctor Slaughter has a few things to go over with you for your mission so please extend to her the same courtesy you would give me."

"Thanks, General Ryan," she said. "First off, I should tell you that I head up one of the R&D branches at Fort Harmony. Unfortunately, I wasn't at the base when this incident occurred. Otherwise, maybe none of this would have been necessary. Are there any questions before I continue?"

"Ma'am," Warrant cut in.

"Yes?"

"Can I speak frankly?"

"Of course."

"Is there a chance that either Cross or I might come into contact with a virus?"

The doctor glanced at the general before answering. "Not exactly."

"Not exactly?" Warrant questioned. "What the hell does that mean?"

The general took over at that point. "What the doctor meant was that there is no chance of you contracting any contagion by being in your fields of operation."

"But there is something out there we should know about, isn't there?" Warrant asked.

"I think…"

"General, I can take it from here," the doctor interrupted. "I understand both of you have the highest security clearance and you both understand anything said here must never leave this room."

We nodded.

"Fort Harmony is just that, a fort. Not only to protect its inhabitants and materials from the outside world but to protect the outside world from us." She continued matter-of-factly. "We are a research and development branch of the military and from time to time we work on projects that theoretically might pose a danger to the public. That's why we have so many security measures and safeguards in place."

Warrant interrupted, "Spare us the government double-talk and tell us what we need to know."

"Major!" the general cut in.

"It's okay," she said. "Major, to be blunt and to the point, we have six, possibly seven individuals on the loose within a five-mile perimeter of the base with specific knowledge of a crucial project we've been working on. To answer another of your questions, the project and possibly the materials they may be carrying, deal with a specific virus we can't afford to let escape."

"I thought we weren't dealing with a contagion?" I asked.

The general sat down. "There is no risk of contracting this contagion. It's not an airborne virus. That's why we've brought the two of you in. You must terminate the targets from a safe distance."

"How is this virus spread?" I asked.

"Through direct contact with blood."

"Like HIV?"

"Exactly," the doctor answered.

"It wouldn't surprise me to find out HIV was man-made as well," Warrant added.

I ignored Warrant's comment and continued, "What are the symptoms of the virus?"

Once again, the doctor looked at the general. The general answered, "We can't disclose that. It has no bearing on the assignment."

"But you guarantee that we are at no risk of contracting it by being in their proximity?" I asked.

"Not unless you're wounded in some way by the carrier," the doctor commented.

The room grew silent and I looked over at Warrant. As usual, he showed no expression.

"Let's get this show on the road," Warrant said.

CHAPTER TWO

I hadn't heard from Warrant since we lost communications after the explosion. The explosion sounded as if it had come from the direction of Fort Harmony but I had no way of knowing if Warrant was alive or dead. What I did know was one of those things we'd been hunting was now hunting me.

Our last confirmed body count, before we'd lost communications, was five targets terminated. If our intelligence was correct that left one or two still alive. What they were, I couldn't say but they sure weren't human.

The first one I'd come across seemed to be some kind of reptilian creature you'd see in a movie. I spotted it crossing a pond. At first, I didn't think much of it until it left the safety of the water and climbed onto the banks of the shore. It stood up on hind legs and was easily the size of a grown man. I watched it walk the shoreline as if it was looking for something until a sound from the forest spooked it.

I couldn't believe my eyes as I watched the thing spring from its hind legs, a good one hundred feet across the beach. It then slipped into the water and disappeared. The pond wasn't large so I perched myself up into a tree and waited. It was almost thirty minutes before it rose from the depths of the pond and surfaced.

I peered through my rifle's scope and zoomed in on the head protruding from the calm waters of the pond. If it wasn't for the scales and their color, I would have thought it was human. I focused in tighter on the creature. It slowly turned its head and I saw its eyes.

I squeezed off a shot and hit it directly in the forehead. The creature bobbed dead in the water for a minute or two before finally submerging.

My next two encounters had been equally unsettling and I wondered what the hell they were doing on that base.

At the moment I had other things on my mind. I'd only caught a quick glimpse of the creature now tracking me but it resembled a tiger, only not like any tiger I'd ever seen before.

The creature, just like the others, traveled on its hind legs like a man. Yellow and black striped fur covered its massive body. It was much larger than the others I'd faced and much faster. I'd managed to get off one-shot and knew I'd hit it because the thing let out an ear-piercing roar of pain before it disappeared into the brush.

I pursued it for a while but never saw it again. Another thing that struck me as odd was the fact there were no traces of blood anywhere. I continued to search for it until I sensed something following me.

I remembered a spot I'd passed earlier, up on high ground with enough open terrain to prevent a surprise attack. I decided to lead the creature there.

The sun sat low in the late afternoon sky as I reached the top of the hill. I hadn't seen the strange creature since I'd shot it earlier but I knew it was somewhere out there. Would it wait for the cover of darkness before making its move? With that thought fresh in my mind I rummaged through my gear and pulled out my night vision scope and placed it on the grass beside me. I took a sip of water from the canteen attached to my belt and leaned against a boulder to rest.

There was a strange silence around me and it struck me as odd there weren't any birds chirping. It was as if the place was dead. There was still enough light to use my regular scope so I lifted my rifle and scanned the area below and around me.

There was nothing.

The tree line at the bottom of the hill loomed ominously, the shadows stretching out towards me as the sun set deeper into the evening sky.

As I peered through my scope, the sound of snapping branches caught my attention. I swung my rifle to the left, towards where the sound had come from but I couldn't make out a thing.

Was it watching me, I wondered?

I lowered my rifle and took in the area around me. There was one solitary tree a few feet from the boulder and it marked the highest point of the hill. It gave me an idea but I'd have to wait until dark.

A horrific roar pierced the quiet and actually made me jump, something I hadn't done since boot camp. The roar trailed off, followed by movement in the woods below. As suddenly as it had started it stopped. The thought it might be playing with me came to mind but I couldn't be sure of what its intentions were.

I paced off the top of the hill so I'd be familiar with it after dark. I also wanted whatever was down there to see me, in hopes of drawing it out while there was still light. Whatever it was didn't take the bait.

The darkness of night finally arrived. I didn't waste time and quickly began to dig out clothes from my gear bag. I assembled a dummy of myself and placed it against the boulder which I'd used as my base for the afternoon. Satisfied it was as good as it was going to get, I pulled a knife from my sheath and ran the blade against my left hand, slicing a thin cut from my thumb to my pinkie. It stung at first but it was bearable. I had no idea if the creature had a keen sense of smell but I couldn't take the chance.

I wiped the fresh blood strategically over the dummy and patched the wound up as best I could.

I grabbed my gear and crept away towards the tree. I stopped to listen again but there wasn't a sound. Whatever was down there was patient. With the aid of my night scope, I searched the area along the tree line below but saw nothing move.

I crouched against the tree and waited.

CHApTER THREE

I thought about my son as I waited in the dark for the creature to reappear. I wondered what he was doing and if he'd had a good day at school. I didn't get to see him often since his mother and I divorced over a year ago. I thought about him a lot though. He was the spitting image of me and I knew it drove Tara nuts.

Tara and I split up soon after I was discharged from the army. She of course had no idea of the reason for my discharge. As far as she was concerned, I was simply a failure at everything I did, with no ambition.

I guess it didn't matter, we never really got along anyway.

I missed my son. I picked Ben up every other weekend and we'd go out and have fun together. Sometimes we'd check out a movie, other times, just hang out and throw the football around. Lately, he'd been asking to go out to the driving range to hit a few golf balls and I promised him we would. The thought I might not see him again or be able to fulfill my promise ate at me.

A faint growl from somewhere below broke me from my thoughts. I pressed myself against the tree and crouched silently, listening. A slight wind picked up and made it hard to pinpoint exactly where the growl had come from. I strained my eyes in the nonexistent light. Only a sliver of a moon hung in the night sky. My fingers tapped against the rifle, a nervous reaction I had since childhood.

The rustling of bushes sounded to my left. I lifted my rifle as a dark form emerged from the tree line. I watched it carefully but decided not to use the night scope just yet. It moved along the tree line slowly. I followed it with my gaze until it disappeared back into the bushes. Had it seen me, I wondered?

A creature suddenly broke from the tree line with incredible speed. From instinct, I had my rifle up and pointed in its direction immediately. My right eye pressed against the scope as I tried to get a fix on it. The creature only made it halfway up the hill before it turned and sprang back down, quickly disappearing back into the woods.

I had a new problem. The creature I'd just seen wasn't the same one that had tracked me earlier. The darkness made it hard to see clearly but I would have sworn the thing resembled an insect of some kind. So where was the other one?

More rustling started along the tree line, this time further to my right. I watched carefully for anything to break from the darkness but nothing did. Whatever was down there seemed content to just crash through the underbrush.

I stretched my legs in an attempt to prevent them from falling asleep. The night air turned cold and I began to see my breath. That was the last thing I needed. Plumes of hot air would give away my location in no time. I pulled my sweater up over my chin and mouth to filter out any telltale exhales and continued to wait.

It wasn't long before the insect creature showed itself. It again quietly walked out from the tree line and moved slowly along the bottom of the hill. I silently lifted my rifle and fixed a bead on it with my scope. I was no expert on the insect world but the first two images that came to mind were ants and grasshoppers. The thing resembled a blend of the two. I continued to watch it slowly climb the hill. I didn't think it saw me but if it did, it pretended not to. It seemed to be trying to flank the dummy I'd put out earlier. I had it clear in my sights and my instincts said to fire but I felt something was wrong. I just didn't know what.

The tiger creature sprang from somewhere behind me. It flew by me with amazing speed. It went by so close to me that I could smell its fur. Instinctively, I dropped and rolled away from the creature until I was back in a crouching position and ready to fire. The two creatures were on the dummy I'd laid out and were tearing it apart. I realized it wouldn't be long before they realized it wasn't real and started to look for me. I decided not to fire because they were too close. If I hit one of them the other one would be on my position in seconds. Too risky.

I snatched my bag, slung my rifle over my back and back stepped down the opposite side of the hill. The whole way down I kept an eye out for something to appear over the top of the hill.

I made it to the tree line without incident and eased into the woods. As quietly as I could I pushed through the dense bush. When I thought I was far enough in, I searched through my gear bag and pulled out a flashlight. I covered the light with my hand and allowed only enough light to escape so I could see my immediate surroundings.

I spotted a path to my right. I took the chance and ran as fast as I could along it, hoping to get as much distance as I could between me and those creatures. I didn't know where I was going but my best guess told me if I continued in this direction, it would bring me closer to Fort Harmony. Somewhere I wasn't sure I wanted to go.

My lungs burned as I stopped to take a rest. I let myself collapse onto the hard-packed earth, taking deep breaths as I laid there. The forest was still and I wondered where the creatures were. I hadn't heard them following me but that meant nothing. I'd been running so hard over the last half an hour; it would have been easy for anything to follow me without being noticed.

My surroundings were pitch-black and I could barely see more than a few feet ahead of me. I lifted myself into a crouching position and listened. It was almost too quiet. I guessed Harmony was only another half-hour walk from where I was. If I could make it there, I might find some help or at least some answers.

I dug into my bag and felt around for the flashlight again. My hand struck its handle and I lifted it out. I continued crouching with the flashlight in my hand, unsure if I should turn it on again or not. I decided to wait a moment and listen some more. The wind died down and there was barely a sound. I used the time to attach my night scope.

Maybe I'd lost them?

I played with the flashlight in my hands until I felt ready.

I turned on the light.

The monstrous head of the tiger-like creature stared at me, unblinking, from the darkness of the forest. I instantly turned the light off, dropped the flashlight into my bag and swung my rifle around. I stared through the night vision scope but the creature was gone. I cursed myself and quickly picked up my bag and began sidestepping down the path. The sound of branches snapping told me something was moving parallel to me.

Had the two creatures separated or were they still together? My question was answered when I heard something move off to my right. I'd been flanked on both sides. I resisted my gut instincts and instead of running, I paused. Slowly I backed up and moved away from the sounds.

After I'd walked a safe distance I stopped, laid down on my stomach and with my rifle lifted, I waited. I could still hear them in the distance crashing through the woods. I breathed a sigh of relief when I realized they weren't coming my way but instead were continuing ahead. I had a good sightline and anything that popped out of the woods would be clearly in my sights.

I waited.

It didn't take long for the first one to emerge from the shadows. It was the insect creature. I had a perfect shot lined up as it stood in the open, seemingly confused. I wanted to fire but waited instead, hoping the tiger creature would show itself as well.

Finally, it did. I watched with interest as neither of the creatures attempted to communicate with the other. The tiger towered over the insect as they took in their surroundings. I wondered if they were able to see any better than I could in the dark that engulfed us?

It was so quiet I was hesitant to pull the trigger and break the silence but if I waited much longer there was a chance they'd disappear again into the woods.

I targeted the tiger in my crosshairs first. I steadied my aim and squeezed off a shot. I don't know if it heard me or if it was pure instinct but it moved suddenly taking the bullet in the back instead of in the head as I'd aimed for. The force of the bullet swung it around and threw it to the ground. The insect, surprised, turned towards me, opening its strange jaws as if to scream something at me. My second bullet didn't miss its mark and the insect's head exploded. I watched the rest of its body collapse to the ground in a heap.

I searched the area for the fallen tiger but it was gone. How could anything have survived that shot, I wondered in dismay.

I wasn't sure if I should move forward or not. I knew there wasn't anything for me back where I'd come from but the thought of the creature waiting for me up ahead wasn't much of a selling point either. I knew I couldn't stay put so I decided to move forward.

I crept slowly at first, listening for anything out of the ordinary. I stayed on the path trying to make as little noise as possible. I wondered if Warrant was out there somewhere going through the same thing as me. He was a survivor so I imagined he was still alive. I thought about using one of my emergency flares in an attempt to contact him but decided it would only give my position away to those creatures.

Warrant had been one of my first pupils. He was a natural marksman. Of all the men I'd trained he was the only one who'd given me a run for my money. The difference between him and I was the fact he liked killing. That was the reason I hadn't picked him for my squad when we went into the jungles of Colombia looking for a drug lord on the lam. I don't think he ever forgave me for that.

The government didn't see it the same way though and gave him his own team. His team had the highest kill ratio of any sniper squad we'd ever had but also the highest mortality rate. Warrant was a risk-taker and to me, that was a liability, not an asset.

I continued down the path, every sense in my body on alert. If the creature was close it didn't seem to want to have another run-in with me any time soon. I stopped every hundred paces or so and did a sweep with my scope but I never spotted it. As I turned a bend in the path, I noticed lights ahead through the trees. I followed the lights as they grew brighter with each step.

The path rose ahead of me and I could feel the strain in my leg muscles. At the top of the small grade, the trees thinned out and I saw the outline of Fort Harmony. The lights from the base cast shadows into the forest and I decided to leave the path and seek the sanctuary of the forest's cover. I pushed myself through the thick underbrush, working my way to the edge of the woods.

I kept in the shadows of the forest as I searched the area around the fort. There didn't seem to be anyone there.

Harmony was much smaller than I'd imagined and was surrounded by a large fence. It didn't take me long to see where the earlier explosion had taken place. One whole corner of the fence was gone and the surrounding ground was heavily scorched. There were no guard towers and I guessed there might have been a guard post where the corner of the fence once stood because there was a dirt road leading up to it. Within the compound sat one lonely two-story warehouse building, nothing else.

The complex didn't seem like much of a high-security operation to me but from past experiences, I knew looks could be deceiving. After I felt safe that I was alone, I crept up to the tree line for a better look. I took off my night scope and replaced it with one that had higher magnification.

Through my lens, I searched the base carefully. Nothing moved. Where was everyone? I found the lack of vehicles strange as well, considering where the base was located. Had everyone fled after the accident?

I studied the lone building carefully, surprised to see the windows which I'd originally thought were real were nothing more than painted murals. The building, made of solid poured concrete stood like a sentry inside the compound. I couldn't even make out an entranceway. I must be facing the back of the building, I decided. I followed the tree line and worked my way around to the front of the building for a better look.

There wasn't a path to follow along the tree line so I forced my way through the underbrush the best I could, making more noise than I wanted. As I moved forward I kept an eye on the building. I could see the side of the building now and it looked exactly like the back.

Something moved but then disappeared behind what I guessed must be the front of the building. I'd only caught it out of the corner of my eye but I was sure I saw something. I stopped moving and watched carefully for any further movement.

None came.

I continued to push through the forest wondering if what I saw was human or one of those creatures?

The side of the building was much longer than I'd thought. I felt tired from fighting my way through the bush and thought about cutting through the yard instead.

Snap.

There was something behind me. I crouched down and grabbed my rifle. I cursed myself for not putting the night scope back on.

Snap.

This time the sound was closer. I risked having my rifle out of commission while I changed scopes but I had to know what was out there. Once my scope was in place, I searched the area. The green-lit images showed nothing but boulders and trees.

Snap.

I spun around to my right and a blurred image passed my sights. I followed its direction and gasped. Staring at me was the tiger but this time it had two other creatures with it. Before I had a chance to do anything it roared and charged towards me.

I fired off a shot and broke from the tree line into the open space that surrounded the base. I knew the bag and rifle were slowing me down but they were all I had to keep me alive. From behind me, more crashing alerted me the creatures were getting closer.

I was still at least a couple of hundred paces from the corner of the building when I looked back and saw the creatures break from the forest. Their snarls and roars echoed against the walls in front of me.

I pushed my legs to move faster but exhaustion from the day's events slowed me down.

I took one last look behind me and realized I wasn't going to make it to the building before them. I had only one chance and it was fifty/fifty at best. I pulled my scope off the rifle and threw it to the ground. I knew the night scope would be useless with all the bright lights surrounding me. I slowed down and when I thought the time was right, I threw myself to the ground and tried to spin around so I'd be facing my attackers.

I miscalculated and hit the ground too hard, throwing the rifle from my grip. I watched in horror as it skidded out of reach.

I tried to make a dive for it but one of the creatures sprang through the air and beat me to it. The creature kicked my rifle away and stared at me menacingly, its yellow eyes gleaming.

Trapped between the creatures and the building, I had no-where to go. I scurried backward with my heels and the palm of my hands until my back pressed up against the side of the building.

The three creatures seemed to study me as they moved slowly towards my position. I noticed two wounds on the tiger which I guessed were the ones I'd inflicted. One was an exit wound just below the shoulder; the other had been a hit to the hip. Neither were bleeding but both wounds were ugly and red which told me the creature was made of flesh and not invincible.

The three of them spread out and encircled me. They began to close in with the tiger leading the other two. The one to my left looked like a snake man, the type you used to see in the freak show at the circus. The one on my right was covered with feathers but had only malformed wings and I doubted it could fly.

The tiger let out a roar and bared its grotesque teeth and fangs as it lunged for me. I reached for the knife I had sheathed at my side and pulled it out. If I was about to die, I wasn't going down without a fight.

A shot rang out and the tiger's head whipped back at an unnatural angle. I watched in surprise as its body lifted from the ground and flew backward, crashing to the ground with a thud. The snake man spun around with incredible agility, looking for the attacker. The feathered creature didn't stick around but instead darted away as if in a panic. It didn't get far before it too took a hit and went down.

The snake man kept looking back and forth between me and the corner of the building and I thought I heard it hiss as a figure came into view.

Warrant kept his rifle aimed straight at the creature as he walked steadily towards it.

"You okay?" he called out, still pointing his rifle at the creature.

"I'm fine," I yelled back. The creature turned to me and hissed as it began to back away. I didn't take my eyes off it.

The thing kept backing away, looking from me to Warrant. When I felt it was far enough away, I slowly got up and went for my rifle. The creature sprang suddenly in my direction. A burst of machine gunfire tore the creature to pieces before my eyes. I looked at its carcass, stunned and turned to Warrant who seemed equally surprised.

I scanned the area around me and saw three figures emerge from the tree line beyond. They ran towards us.

"Who's in command here?" one of them shouted, between large drags of air.

Warrant and I looked at each other.

"Are there more of them around?" the same one asked.

Warrant stepped towards the three of them as I picked up my rifle. "No idea," he answered, "but I don't think so."

The shortest of the three approached us. "Are you two from this base?" he asked. "Are there any others alive?"

I let Warrant do the talking. "We're not from the base," he answered. "I only got here thirty minutes ago and my friend over there," he pointed at me, "just arrived, but found it necessary to bring some unwanted guests with him."

"If you're not from the base, what are you doing here?" The man was now close enough for me to notice his sergeant stripes.

"I might ask the same of you," Warrant added, "but since we're all in an awkward situation here, there's no time to play games. I'm Major Warrant and this civilian is James Cross."

"You're snipers," the sergeant cut in. "I've heard your names before."

"We are and I'm guessing you're part of the company who's supposed to be holding the perimeter five miles away from here. So, what are you doing here? Get lost?"

The three men shuffled their feet for a moment and seemed unsure what to do. I guessed the sergeant was the leader of the trio. The tallest and heaviest of the three had corporal's stripes and the third lanky one had a corporal's rank as well.

"Our lines are broken," the sergeant said finally. "Everything is a mess. We've lost our commander and most of the men are dead or turned."

I cut in. "Turned?"

"Yeah, didn't you know?" the sergeant asked, astonished.

"Know what?" Warrant asked.

The three of them looked at one another as if we were from another planet. The sergeant sank to the ground and put his head into his hands. The tall corporal stepped up and said, "If they wound you and draw blood, you're dead."

"But not for long," the lanky corporal added.

"You're not making sense," I said.

The sergeant, still on the ground with his head hung down, turned to me. "It's true. Whatever these things are, they can turn you into one of them just by scratching you."

"You've got to be shitting me," Warrant said as he looked over at me.

"I wish I were," the sergeant replied.

"So, tell us what happened out there," I asked.

"It's a mess," the sergeant started. "We were guarding the line, like you said, about five miles back." He paused. "They came out of nowhere. Faster and more vicious than anything I've ever seen."

Warrant and I stared at him as he paused.

"Go on," I told him.

"Well, after the first attack was over, we thought we'd re-pelled them. We had a lot of wounded but no casualties. Most of the wounds were only superficial. We set up a field hospital to tend to the wounded. But no sooner had we set it up, they hit us again. This time doing more damage because our lines were so thinned out."

"So how did you hold on?" I asked.

"As best we could," he answered. "After the second attack, we had even more wounded plus a few dead. When we got them to the field hospital we found that many of the previously wounded had come down with a fever."

"Fever?" I asked.

The sergeant seemed at a loss. His eyes looked tired and had a lost look to them. "I know it sounds insane," he said, "but they all came down with it."

"Were you able to evacuate them out?" Warrant asked.

"No," the sergeant answered. "We called for support and im-mediate evacuation of our wounded but it was refused."

"Refused? Why?" I said, not believing what I'd heard.

"That's not the worst of it," the sergeant said.

"It gets worse?" I asked.

"Much worse," the sergeant answered. "Our wounded started to turn into the same damn monsters who'd attacked us."

"How's that possible?" I asked.

"That's what we came here to find out," he said, getting to his feet.

All five of us stood quietly. I couldn't believe what I was hear-ing but if I'd tried to explain to anyone what I'd seen, they'd have thought I was crazy.

A sudden blast of machine gunfire caught our attention. I could tell it was from far-off in the distance but that didn't reassure me. We looked at one another as if for an answer to the nightmare we'd all found ourselves sharing.

"Are the lines still holding?" Warrant asked.

"No." The sergeant said.

The tall corporal cut in, "All hell broke loose on their fifth at-tack. While we were trying to fight them off, we began to be attacked by our own men. Men who'd transformed into the same creatures we'd been fighting." The corporal stopped as if he couldn't go on thinking about it.

"That's when the lines finally broke and we were unable to contain the creatures anymore," the sergeant added. "It was everyone for themselves at that point."

"How did you three manage to survive?" Warrant asked them.

"My lieutenant ordered me to try to contact Fort Harmony and find out what we were up against and to get help," the sergeant explained. "I found Adams here first," he said, pointing at the tall corporal. "Richards, we came across later, cornered by some Bigfoot. Adams gunned it down the same way he did that one." He motioned toward the snake man lying dead on the ground.

"And the three of you made it here alone?" I asked.

"Wasn't too hard," the sergeant said. "I think most of the creatures are moving away from here and towards the perimeter. At least that's my guess because we never came across another one until we finally made it here."

I mulled over what they'd said before I spoke. It all sounded so preposterous but the doctor had said the virus was transferred through contact with blood. So what they said did make sense. "I can assume then that the creatures have broken through the lines and are outside the perimeter?"

"Yes," the sergeant answered.

"Any idea how many we'd be looking at?" I asked.

"Hundreds, if you count the wounded who've turned."

We grew silent again as the number sunk in.

I looked away and took in my surroundings. The base was well lit, which meant their power was still functioning and other than the hole in the fence, everything else seemed to be intact. But where were the people?

"What about you two?" the sergeant asked, interrupting my train of thought. "How did you get here?"

Before I could answer, Warrant spoke up, "We made our way here from a drop zone, on orders to do reconnaissance and report back on what we found."

"So you have contact with headquarters?" one of the corporals said, sounding relieved.

"No," Warrant answered. "We lost communications hours ago.

"That's great," the corporal said.

"Did you know what you were getting into before you dropped?" the sergeant asked.

This time I answered, "No, we're as blind as you."

"Enough small talk," Warrant interrupted. "The power is still operational here so I'd guess communications are as well. I think we should check it out unless anyone has a better idea?"

No one did. Without another word, we followed Warrant who had already disappeared around the corner.

As I tagged along behind the rest of the men I heard the two corporals speaking in hushed tones.

"Do you buy their story?"

"Of course not, they're Special Ops and killers to boot. I'd doubt they'd tell us shit."

"What do you think they're doing then?"

"They probably came here to clean up the mess. I imagine they've been here longer than they admit and probably took out everyone they found alive here."

"But why?"

"To cover it all up of course. Use your head, idiot."

Before their conversation could continue they stopped dead in their tracks and I almost walked into them. I followed their gaze and saw the gaping hole in the front of the building. Bodies littered the yard around it. What changed the scene from horrifying to terrifying though was on closer inspection I noticed the bodies had all died of self-inflicted wounds.

"Welcome to Hell's Gate, gentlemen," Warrant said. "Let's go have a look inside."

Chapter Four

The hole in the building was enormous. In addition to the dead bodies there were crows flying ominously overhead.

The smell of burned materials hung in the air like a warning to stay out. I followed Warrant in while the other three lagged behind us. More bodies lay strewn along the hallway. Some had ugly gashes across their bodies. Blood covered almost everything. No matter how badly mangled they were, each body shared one thing in common with the next. They'd all been shot.

The hallway looked like any other you'd find in an industrial complex, minus the dead bodies. The same bland walls, the same tiled floors. The clock on the wall had a round face with large numbers. I checked it with my watch and found it was accurate. We navigated our way down the hall being careful not to step on any of the bodies. A few doors lined the hallway as we passed but we didn't bother to open them and look inside.

Around the first corner, there were fewer bodies. Only two to be exact and around the next there were none. Power was still fully functional so there were no dark corners for a creature to lurk in but it didn't make me feel any safer. With each room we passed my mind turned to one big question. What went on behind those closed doors? That question would have to wait, our main objective was to find some way of communicating with the outside world and to get some help.

I knew Warrant was leading us to the center of the complex. The base of communications was almost always found in the center of a building for maximum protection and security.

"What do you think?" I asked Warrant.

He turned to me and glanced over my shoulder before answering, "Looks deserted."

"Did you notice the Coup de Grace shot on those bodies back there?"

"Kind of hard to miss," he answered.

I looked back at the trio behind us and they appeared to be keeping their distance from us. "Think they picked up on it?" I asked.

"I doubt they'd be able to pick out an apple tree in an orchard."

"What'll we do if the base's communications are down?"

Warrant smiled. "We'll worry about that when the time comes." He turned away and continued walking down the hall.

Warrant stopped in front of two large metal doors. I stopped a few feet away and signaled for those following to hold up. I watched Warrant try the handles and was surprised when the doors opened easily. He disappeared into the room. I followed and heard the footsteps of the others following behind me.

The room was much smaller than I'd expected. Computers lined the walls but in the corner sat a switchboard, still lit up. Warrant walked towards the switchboard as I had a look at the monitors. All of them had their screen savers on but with a move of the mouse, they burst back to life. I noticed half-full coffee cups and partially eaten food littered around the place. Whatever happened had happened fast.

"They're still working," Warrant told me, picking up a headset.

I walked towards him. "Can you get through?"

"I'm trying now."

I waited patiently and grabbed a seat. The other three stood quietly by the door. "Why don't you three take a load off?" I said.

Before they could answer Warrant cut in, "I think I've got a line out." He paused to listen through his headset. "Yeah, it's ringing." I noticed the faintest smiles appear on the trio's faces for the first time since we'd hooked up.

"Tell them to get a chopper in here quick and get us the hell out," Richards said. Warrant ignored him.

"Patch me through to General Ryan, it's an emergency." Warrant ordered into the headset.

Being cynical, the first thought to go through my mind was to wonder if he was faking the conversation for the benefit of our three friends. I decided that probably wasn't the case since I'd never known Warrant to care for anyone else's feelings before.

"I don't care if he's busy, interrupt him. Tell him, the Spider and the Mongoose have entered the nest." Warrant looked at his watch as he waited.

"I don't think Ryan's going to like what you're about to tell him," I said.

"I think you're right," he answered. He was about to say something else when he gripped the headset tighter to his ear. "Yes sir, that's correct."

I watched Warrant carefully as he gave cryptic answers to the General.

"No, sir," he paused. "Yes. No, no visible survivors, sir."

"One moment sir." He motioned for me to come over. "Have a pen handy?" he asked me. I grabbed one from the counter beside me and pushed it towards him with a small pad of paper.

"Go ahead, sir." He scribbled something down on the piece of paper. "ETA sir? Understood, sir. Mongoose out."

All eyes were on Warrant as he hung up.

"What's the word?" I asked.

"Get over here," Warrant ordered the three soldiers. "We won't bite."

The three of them sheepishly walked towards us. Warrant didn't wait for them to get to us before he started, "That was

General Ryan. A chopper will be here in exactly one hour to pick us up."

"An hour?" Adams cut in. "Where the hell are they, the North Pole?"

"An hour is exactly how long they've given us to complete our new mission."

I looked at him questioningly but didn't say anything. I didn't have to because Adams spoke up first. "What new mission?"

"The General has ordered us to find a laptop."

"A laptop?" Adams asked sarcastically, "You've got to be shitting me?"

Warrant ignored him and looked at me. "Think you can keep these three alive for another hour?"

"Where are you planning to be?"

"It'll be quicker if I go and find it alone."

"I don't think so," I said. "If something happens to you along the way there has to be a backup."

"Since when do I ever need backup?"

"We're coming," I stated.

Warrant didn't say a word. He tossed the headset onto the counter, pushed through the trio and headed for the door.

The five of us walked down the hallway. The sound of our boots hitting the tiled floor echoed off the nondescript walls. We turned a corner and noticed the change in lighting ahead.

We halted immediately.

"Cross, take point," Warrant ordered. "You wanted to come along, so go check out what happened to the lights up there."

I wanted to say something but didn't bother. I replaced my rifle with a sidearm and slowly walked down the hall towards the gloom. I didn't look back but instead kept my eyes glued towards the upcoming corner. The hallway got darker with every step. I reached the corner and tried to peer around it but couldn't make out a thing in the darkness. I backed against the far wall and slid myself along it until I faced the opening to the hallway.

A dim light filtered out from a room about halfway down. I listened for movement but heard nothing. I signaled for the others to follow and continued down the hallway.

A figure appeared out of the darkness, crumpled in a heap against the wall.

I stopped.

I heard a footstep behind me so I raised my hand to signal them to hold tight. Slowly, I walked towards whatever was lying there. I approached it with caution and when I was close enough I kicked it with my foot. It didn't move. I kicked it again. Still nothing.

"What is it?" Warrant called out, startling me.

I didn't answer. I kicked at it one more time and satisfied it wasn't alive I pushed it over until it was lying face-up.

The thing was hideous. It wasn't one of the creatures but it didn't seem human either, except for its shape. It was as if the face had melted and then become swollen. The body stank of something I couldn't put my finger on. I felt a sudden presence beside me and spun around but it was only Warrant.

"Looks like we have a new mystery on our hands," he said. "What do you think happened to him?"

"No idea," I answered him.

Warrant looked over his shoulder at the other three who'd hung back and called out an order, "You three, check inside that room and see if anything is interesting in there."

The three of them didn't jump to command but instead reluctantly moved forward and disappeared into the room.

"What else did Ryan tell you?" I asked. I peeked into the room and watched Adams look through some cabinets as I waited for Warrant's reply.

"He gave me a code to a safe."

"Did he say what was in the safe?"

"All he said was, there's a laptop in the safe and I'm to bring it with us to the pick-up."

"And where is this safe?" I asked.

Warrant pointed at the floor. "Underneath us, one floor below." He grinned.

I checked my watch. "We better get going then. We've already wasted fifteen minutes of our hour."

Warrant faced the doorway. "Time to move out," he told them.

"Take a look at this," a voice said from inside the room. It sounded like the sergeant. I walked into the room and saw them all staring at something on a table. As I approached the group they parted and I saw what they were looking at. It was a dissection table and on top of it lay a creature that seemed half man, half fish. I didn't know which. It was cut open from chest to belly, exposing everything its insides had to offer.

"My God, they must have been experimenting on these creatures in here," the sergeant said, holding back a gag.

The only thought I had at the moment was to question what kind of a world I'd brought my son into.

"Cover him and let's move out," Warrant ordered.

No one needed any convincing so we exited the room and followed the hallway further into the darkness. Warrant pulled a flashlight from his bag and flashed it down the dark hall, lighting our way. He aimed the beam of light at the wall and the ceiling. The lightbulb which had once lit this part of the hallway was shattered and bullet holes riddled the area around it.

"Looks like we had a firefight," Warrant commented.

I thought about that for a minute before speaking. "The staff from the base must have tried to make a stand to try to keep the creatures contained."

"Doesn't seem like it worked," he answered.

"No, no it doesn't." I ran my fingers through my hair and let out a deep breath. "What do you think was going on here?"

"I have no idea and I don't care," he told me a matter-of-factly. "What I do know is, I want to get that laptop and get the hell out of here."

"Just shoot them and bag them, eh Warrant?"

He gave me one of those grins I hated and said, "That's right. If it makes you feel any better, it looks to me like they're working on creating some kind of human hybrid."

"We don't have that kind of technology," I said.

"Says who?" He stared at me with that grin again. "You think they're aliens from outer space?"

"I didn't say that."

"Then what do you think?"

"I don't know but I think we should check around some more and try to find out what the hell is going on."

Warrant played with his flashlight. "That wasn't one of our orders."

"I don't give a shit about the orders."

"You want to risk being left behind?" he asked. "Let's just get the laptop and get out of here. Then you can do all the snooping you want on your own time."

I looked away from him in disgust and noticed the weapons that were now pointed at us.

I'd almost forgotten about our three friends but they had my full attention now. Warrant must have noticed my tenseness because he turned around to see what I was staring at.

"What are you men doing?" Warrant asked with authority.

"We want to know what's going on?" the sergeant answered. "We're sick of the secrecy and bullshit around here. We want some answers."

"What makes you think we have any answers?" I asked.

Richards spoke up first, "We know who you are and what you do. How do we know you two don't have plans to eliminate any loose ends?"

"You've watched too many movies," Warrant said with a chuckle.

"Maybe so but I don't want to take any chances."

"So, what are you going to do? Shoot us?" Warrant asked.

"Not unless we have to," Richards answered. "It's nothing personal."

"That's a relief," Warrant said almost laughing at them.

I wondered if I could make it around the corner without getting shot but who knew what might be waiting around the corner in the darkness. "Let's all be calm," I said. "What exactly do you have in mind?"

The three of them looked at one another and I wondered who the ringleader was.

The sergeant spoke first and I was relieved because he seemed the most levelheaded of the three. "I'm sorry about this but you have to understand where we're coming from. This whole thing is a fucking mess and we just want to get out of here alive."

Warrant was about to speak but I cut him off because I knew he'd just make matters worse. "That's fine," I said encouragingly. "Did you have a plan in mind?"

The sergeant looked nervous. "Not really," he answered. "We'll stick with you two but you stay in front of us and we'll cover your backs.

"That's reassuring," Warrant said with a laugh.

I glared at him but he just smiled back. "Okay, that's fine," I offered. "I'll be straight with you. We have to go underground. We've been ordered to retrieve a laptop somewhere on the floor below."

"What's down there?" Adams asked.

"We don't know. All we know is there's a safe with a laptop and Warrant has the code to get into it."

"Then what?"

"Simple, we open the safe, take the laptop and rendezvous with our ride out of here."

The three of them spoke with one another in hushed tones.

Warrant leaned towards me and said, "We should grease them all."

"Shut up for once," I told him.

The trio broke up and the sergeant said, "All right."

Before I could reply Warrant cut in, "You girls done talking now? If so let's move out, we're running out of time."

The general must have given Warrant directions when they were on the phone because he seemed to know exactly where to go. We followed him along corridor after corridor, each peppered with gunshot holes and blood-soaked walls. We discovered bodies strewn in horrible poses along the way.

I began to find it odd that everybody we came across had one single bullet shot to the head. At first, I thought they might have been self-inflicted but few had weapons by their side. So who had shot them and where were they now?

We reached a large bulky metal door and found it ajar. Warrant had the sergeant and Richards pull it open. The entrance opened to stairs which led down into the bowels of the building.

"Who wants to go first?" Warrant asked.

"This is your show, Major, after you," the sergeant replied.

"Coming?" Warrant asked me.

"You can take point this time," I said.

Warrant nodded and entered the stairwell. It was well lit and I thanked God for small mercies. Down we went until we came to another metal door, this time wide open.

"Make sure you're locked and loaded and watch each other's backs," I told them. We entered a hallway marked "High-Security Floor NC. NC Level Cardholders Only," in bright red and yellow letters.

Everything seemed too peaceful.

We pressed on, our weapons ready for anything that might spring out at us. We turned the first corner and I couldn't believe my eyes. A window, almost the entire length of the hallway stood before us. On the other side of the window was a large room. We stood in horror at the sight. Rows upon rows of creatures lay on tables from one end of the room to the other. It was like looking through a window of a maternity ward for monsters.

None of the creatures seemed to be conscious but each had a tube inserted into their neck. A quick calculation told me there were close to fifty of them in there. I wondered if there were other rooms like this one elsewhere in the building.

"Let's kill them all while they're asleep," Adams suggested.

"No," Warrant told him, "we can't risk anything until after we've recovered the laptop."

"Fuck the laptop," Richards spoke up. "These things could be waiting for us when we come back if we don't deal with them now."

Warrant looked over at me. "What do you think?"

"I say chance it and leave them be. They seem under control in there and I don't see any reason why they'd suddenly wake up if they haven't yet." I tried to gauge our three friends' reactions but it didn't look favorable.

"Cross is right," the sergeant piped up. "If we try to engage them now it could wake the others up before we can get to them all."

Adams and Richards looked unsure. I kept my eye on Richards in case he tried to do anything stupid. Adams eased the tension when he sided with the sergeant forcing Richards to go along.

"Now that's settled let's get moving," Warrant said.

We followed two more hallways but never saw another room like the first one. We finally stopped at a door marked "Colonel Paterson."

"Is this it?" I asked.

"This is it," Warrant replied, trying the doorknob. It was locked. Warrant stepped back and kicked the door and it sprang open. We pointed our weapons into the opening. Seated behind a large mahogany desk was Colonel Paterson or so his name badge told us. In his right hand he held the gun I guessed that he had used it to take his own life. On closer inspection, we noticed the neat little hole in the right side of his head, just above his ear. The left side of his head was a mangled mess and I looked away.

"This place is totally fucked up," Richards said. "You know what it must mean if the Colonel blew his own brains out?"

"Yeah, we're screwed," Adams answered.

The sergeant lowered his weapon. "What do you two make of this?" he asked.

I said nothing, figuring Warrant would have something to say as usual but he didn't. We looked around as if pretending the body of the dead colonel wasn't there. As I looked down at the colonel's desk, I noticed a ledger which had a pen neatly lain across it. I picked it up and opened it.

"Look at this," I called out, holding the ledger up.

"What is it?" asked Warrant as the other three gathered around.

"Looks like the colonel's personal diary," I answered. With the group of them looking over my shoulder I opened it up to the last page.

I fear no one will ever have the chance to read this but if these notes are found I pray it's because you've found a way to undo what we've done here.

Over the last eighteen hours, we've learned these creatures are not the mindless things we'd bred them to be. I and a handful of men have survived the initial attack and have barricaded ourselves down here. We managed to execute all wounded personnel before being driven downstairs, may God forgive us.

In our vain attempt to play God we've created our own undoing. Just the other day we were celebrating our genius when we'd thought we'd finally made a breakthrough but it was not to last. Our inability to teach them to communicate was a major setback.

Unknown to us, the creatures could indeed communicate and did so through a form of telepathy we were unaware of and which they'd kept hidden from us. When we realized our folly it was too late. Their attacks were quick and merciless and their ranks swelled as our wounded transformed into their kind within minutes. All hope is lost for the few of us remaining and I can only hope and pray that they can be contained before it's too late.

I can hear gunfire out in the corridor, they must have finally broken through. Whoever reads this, please tell my wife and my daughter Ginny that I'm sorry and I love them.

"That's it?" Adams questioned. "There's no mention of how to deal with them?"

"Apparently not," I said.

"That's just great," Adams added. "Now we find out these monsters can communicate through telepathy? What's next?"

Warrant came forward and stared at each of us. "Enough," he ordered. "Let's get the laptop and head for the rendezvous point." He left us standing there and walked towards a painting of a seashore. He ripped it off the wall, exposing the safe behind it. He quickly punched in some numbers and opened the safe. We held our breath until we saw Warrant pull out the laptop.

"Let's get the hell out of here," the sergeant said.

As we filtered out of the office, leaving the colonel in his subterranean resting place, I noticed we were missing a man.

"Where's Richards?" I asked.

Everyone looked around as if they'd find him hiding behind some of the furniture but he was gone.

"Come on," Warrant ordered. He took off down the corridor with the laptop safely snuggled under his arm like a football. This time we weren't trying to hide our whereabouts and our heavy footsteps echoed through the corridors.

"Do you see him?" I called out to Warrant, just a few steps ahead of me.

"No," he answered. He stopped suddenly and put up his hand.

We were at the large window.

Richards stood in the middle of the room filled with creatures on tables. We watched him pull the tubing from the necks of the unconscious creatures as we stood there motionless. None of the creatures moved and I felt a rush of relief wash over me. I didn't relish the idea of being trapped in this ungodly subterranean house of horrors if they were all awakened.

The sergeant entered the room first. "What the hell do you think you're doing?" he yelled out at Richards.

Richards didn't bat an eye but instead continued yanking out the tubes. He looked maniacal in his movements and actions like a man possessed, as he moved from table to table without interruption.

Adams entered the room next and passed the sergeant without a glance. He approached Richards and received no reaction. Richards pressed on. Finally, almost at the back of the room, Adams grabbed Richards's hand and stopped him. Richards pulled back.

"We have to kill them all, don't you see?" he cried out. "There's already too many of them out there. We can't let these things get out as well."

Adams tried to hold him but Richards pulled away before collapsing to his knees, crying. "This is all madness," he shrieked. Adams knelt and managed to put his arm around him and Richards tucked his face into Adam's chest.

I didn't feel comfortable watching this show of emotion so instead, I entered the room and tried to make sense of it all myself. The walls were lined with huge computer banks all blinking and purring away. Giant canisters of all shapes and sizes hung on the walls. The only things the canisters had in common were the bright warning signs on them, indicating which ones were flammable and explosive or which ones contained poisonous chemicals.

My thoughts turned again to any other possible survivors. There should have been some who escaped? Had the others all become the creatures we now stared at?

As I stood thinking, something brushed against my leg. I looked down and saw the arm of one of the creatures dangling from the table. I stepped back and noticed the creature's eyes were open and staring straight at me.

"They're coming to," I yelled out, backing away.

Warrant charged into the room with his weapon ready. "Let's get out of here," he shouted.

Without warning, Richards pushed Adams away from him, drew a knife and began stabbing the creatures.

"Holy shit," the sergeant said under his breath.

I followed his stare and noticed all the creatures were writhing around in pain as if they too had been stabbed. Many attempted to lift themselves from the tables.

"Adams, Richards, get out of there, now," the sergeant ordered.

Richards ignored the order but Adams began running between the tables towards us. He'd only made it halfway when one of the creatures grabbed him and dragged him beneath a table. It wasn't much longer before Richards was also surrounded by them and disappeared beneath their writhing mass.

The sergeant backed into me and the two of us quickly escaped the room.

Warrant stood in the hallway like a statue. "We have to leave them," he said.

I looked through the window and noticed Adams lifting himself from the floor, a bloody knife in his hand. All three of us watched in horror as he struggled to his feet and staggered toward us.

"He's wounded," the sergeant commented. "We have to help him."

"It's too late," Warrant said. "You said it yourself. Even a scratch from one of them can turn you."

"We can't just leave him like that," the sergeant said, emotion clearly audible in his voice.

No sooner had he finished his sentence when a shot rang out. A neat hole appeared in Adams' head and he dropped like a rock. Warrant stood in the doorway of the room with his raised rifle.

"Shoot for the canisters along the walls," I told Warrant. "Maybe we can finish the whole lot of them." Warrant didn't even blink an eye before he tore off two shots. Almost simultaneously the window exploded around us.

The sergeant and I hit the floor hard, pieces of glass and debris striking us from every angle. We both jumped back to our feet immediately, not wanting to be caught off guard by any of the creatures.

I couldn't believe what I saw through the broken window. The creatures were all on fire, some stumbling into one another while others crashed to the ground in burning heaps.

Some of the luckier ones who'd managed to somehow escape the initial blast charged toward us. The sergeant and I opened fire and between the three of us, we managed to put them all down.

The fire began to rage out of control and the heat against our faces grew intense.

"We have to get out of here before the other canisters blow," I shouted over the racket.

We took off at a run and were halfway down the hallway when the next explosion hit. It knocked the three of us to the floor but we scrambled quickly to our feet. We reached the heavy metal door and luckily found it still ajar. We entered the stairwell and it took all three of us to push the door closed.

We raced up the stairs to the main floor, once again shoving the heavy metal door shut.

"Let's get to the rendezvous point," Warrant said.

We ran past the bullet-riddled walls and the blood-soaked hallways. Past the dead and mangled bodies, until we reached the gaping hole where the front entrance had once stood.

Fresh air. I couldn't remember ever enjoying it more. We hadn't even got halfway across the compound when we heard the sound of a helicopter somewhere beyond the tree line. I reached into my bag and pulled out a flare gun, pointed it in the air and fired it off.

"Okay, let's not get sloppy now," Warrant said. "Form a small perimeter and let's watch each other's back. We're almost home."

I faced the building we'd barely escaped from and listened as the sound of the chopper grew closer.

An intense beam of light broke through the trees behind me and I felt the sudden rush of wind blow against my back. I turned and smiled at the sight of the Chinook chopper landing a few hundred yards behind me.

I turned back to continue my watch when I saw the first of the burning creatures lurch from the building. More appeared behind them, many of them still on fire. I heard shouting behind me and turned to see the sergeant and Warrant racing towards the chopper. I quickly left my position and did the same. I didn't look back until I was safely in the helicopter. Warrant handed me a headset so we could communicate.

We lifted from the ground as the creatures continued moving towards us. We opened fire as the chopper hovered over the base until every last one of them lay dead on the ground. We waited for a while circling the building to make sure there were no more of them left standing.

As we continued to hover, I finally noticed the pilot was not alone in the cockpit. Doctor Slaughter was sitting beside him filming the scene with a video camera. My first instinct was to grab her and force her to tell me what the hell she'd done, right before throwing her from the chopper, but I let it pass.

Hovering above the trees the chopper turned and faced the building, allowing the good doctor one last look at her failed project.

To my surprise, the chopper fired off two missiles which exploded in an amazing show of firepower, flattening the building to the ground.

I stared out the window in disbelief as the chopper turned and flew off over the treetops.

Finally, I'd had enough and approached the doctor. "Did we manage to contain them?" I asked.

"No," she said simply.

"What's happening down there?" I asked. "And what are we going to do about this mess?"

"Pray," was all she answered.

CHAPTER FIVE

The helicopter skimmed the treetops as we flew toward the base, the doctor's prophetic words mulling in my mind. The cool night air drifted by and I breathed it in deeply to get rid of the stench of burning flesh which still stuck to me like glue. I used the downtime to take an inventory of my gear and repack my bag. I took out a notepad and scribbled down everything I could remember of the night's events for the briefing I knew would be waiting for me on our arrival back at the base.

The sergeant hadn't said a word since we hopped into the chopper and I guessed he was feeling a bit out of his element. He didn't seem scared and although he never made eye contact with any of us, I could tell he was being careful and taking everything in. I thought he might have made a good sniper. I decided I'd keep an eye on him to make sure he didn't get lost in the shuffle once we arrived at the base.

Warrant kept to himself. I could almost hear the gears grinding away in his mind. I watched him do a quick inventory of his kit and then break down his weapon and put it back together again, over and over. A few times, after he'd completed the process, he'd point the rifle directly at the doctor's head. I couldn't tell if she'd noticed or not but if she had she never let on.

The doctor stared out the window. I would have loved to have known what she was thinking. I studied her as she sat there with the laptop we'd given her and her video camera. She seemed deep in thought. What could be going through the mind of someone who'd just released this kind of horror into the world?

"Doctor Slaughter?"

She turned her head toward me and smiled. The smile sent a shiver down my spine. It was as phony as they came. "Yes?" she answered, still smiling.

"Are there measures in place to handle this kind of situation?"

"Not this far along, no," she replied, still smiling.

I noticed the sergeant watching us closely. Warrant, with his hands still on his rifle, came toward us.

"There has to be some kind of a plan," I said.

She looked back out the window before answering, "All containment methods were lost once they breached the perimeter."

"Bullshit," Warrant said.

"No, sadly enough, it's the truth," she replied.

"They must be setting up another perimeter," I said.

She didn't respond but instead continued to gaze out the window.

"Do we even have a chance at this point?" I asked.

"I don't know," she answered, not looking away from the window.

I tried to calculate in my head how fast these things might spread once they hit populated areas. It occurred to me that after the base, the closest town was Stoneaway Rapids which was where my son lived with his mother. "Have we warned the surrounding communities or tried to evacuate them?" I asked.

"I don't know," she said.

"What do you know?" Warrant piped in.

She ignored him.

"What the hell was the purpose behind creating those things?" I asked.

Slaughter turned to me and gave me that sickening smile again. "That's classified," she answered smugly.

Warrant lifted his rifle and pressed it against her head. "I wouldn't be so smart if I were you," he told her.

"You're smarter than that," she said, turning around in her seat to face him. "I'm the only hope you have right now. No one knows more about them than me. If you kill me, the effects would be disastrous."

"Oh yeah, right," Warrant said sarcastically. "Like things could get worse."

"They can and most likely will before it's over," she told him.

"They're not invincible," I cut in, trying to ease the tension. "They die when they're shot easy enough."

She turned to me. "True, but only a head shot will do it and not everyone is as capable as you and Major Warrant."

I thought about that for a moment. For the average soldier to be able to make a kill shot on something which moved as quickly as these creatures did, it would almost take a miracle. And every wounded soldier who missed would likely become just one more of those creatures.

I had to get to my son.

"Prepare for landing," the pilot told us.

Bright lights, as well as the glowing lights of fires, appeared off in the distance.

"What the hell's going on down there?" the sergeant asked, finally joining the conversation.

We looked ahead as we drew closer to the base. The chopper cleared the tree line and we couldn't believe our eyes. Bodies were everywhere and fires had consumed most of the base's buildings. The helicopter hovered above the scene.

"They couldn't have got here this fast," Warrant pointed out.

"Can you see anyone moving?" the sergeant asked, craning his neck for a better view.

I couldn't but before I could answer the pilot motioned off to his left. "Someone is signaling us," he said, still pointing.

Off to our left a bright white light blinked on and off, on and off. I tapped the pilot on the shoulder. "Take us closer," I told him.

The signaling light came from the top floor of the small airstrip tower. The pilot turned the chopper to our left and we flew toward the tower. As we grew closer, we easily made out figures through the windows.

"Contact them and get the status," I asked.

"We've been ordered to maintain communication silence," the pilot answered.

Warrant turned his rifle away from the doctor and pointed it at the pilot. "A bit late to worry about that now," he said.

The pilot hailed the tower.

We received no reply.

As we descended, Warrant and I opened the side doors of the chopper and covered the landing area with our rifles. I couldn't see any movement and it bothered me.

The helicopter touched down and I jumped out immediately. I ran a few yards ahead until I crouched into a covering position and surveyed the area. The sergeant must have come out next because before I knew it he was beside me in a crouch with his weapon drawn.

"What do you want to do?" the sergeant asked me, shouting over the whooping sounds of the helicopter's blades.

I heard the engine cut off and the breeze from the blades began to let up. "We'll wait for the rest of them and head toward the tower," I answered.

He nodded.

I turned to look for Warrant and saw the pilot jump down from the chopper and hustle towards us. Around the front of the chopper, the doctor and Warrant appeared. They seemed to be in a heated discussion as they moved towards us.

The pilot knelt beside me. "They're going to kill each other," he said, nodding toward Warrant and the doctor.

"Make two less to worry about," I answered with a grin.

The doctor stormed over to me, her face crimson red. "The General will hear about the way I've been treated," she warned us.

"Just hope he's one of the survivors," Warrant told her.

She turned away in a huff and walked briskly toward the tower.

"Hey, hold up," I yelled.

She ignored me.

"Let her be," Warrant said. "Maybe she'll flush out anything that's hiding over there. Better to use her as bait than one of us."

We watched her march across the open expanse of field. She acted like she didn't have a care in the world other than to report us for not treating her properly. We'd see how fast she came running back if one of those things appeared though.

None did.

She disappeared into the hangar below the tower.

The helicopter, now silent, sat exposed behind us. I still had a buzzing in my ears from the flight. "One of us should stay with the chopper," I said. "It may be our only way of escape if things sour."

"I'll stay," the pilot offered. "It's my bird and if things do go bad at least I can have it ready by the time you get back."

I handed him a weapon from my bag. "Take off if it gets too hot down here but make sure you come back for us."

"Will do," he said.

I patted him on the back for good luck and stood up. "Let's move out," I said to the others.

We walked with less purpose than the doctor had and made sure to cover our backs along the way. The tree line which surrounded the base was impenetrable to the eye and I wondered if anything might be watching us from the shadows. The night was deathly silent as we walked towards the hangar. A few yards from the entrance to the hangar we halted.

"What do you think?" I asked Warrant.

"Looks okay," he replied. "We'd have heard her scream if there'd been a problem."

"Not if they got her quickly," I said.

"Send the Sarge in for a look," Warrant suggested.

I ignored him and said, "You two split up and cover the sides of the entrance and I'll go in."

Warrant and the sergeant moved out and took positions on opposite sides of the entrance. When they gave me the all-clear I took a deep breath and headed toward the opening. I looked into the hangar and it seemed clear, but as I walked through the entranceway, I stopped suddenly. Dead bodies filled the place and in the back corner stood what looked like a hastily built triage area.

There were bodies of humans mingled with bodies of the creatures who'd attacked them. More startling were the bodies of things that looked like they'd started to change but never finished their transformation. There was no sign of movement and no sign of the doctor. I sidestepped until I made it to the far wall and had a good position to cover the area around me and signaled the all-clear for the other two.

Warrant and the sergeant scrambled towards me, taking up positions on either side of me.

"Look at this mess," the sergeant commented.

The hangar was the size of a football field. Assorted vehicles and airplanes were lined up in rows. Some of the vehicles still contained bodies, presumably, those who'd tried to escape the carnage but never made it. I spotted a large metal staircase toward the back of the hangar and pointed toward it. "That'll take us to the tower," I said. "We'll keep against the wall and follow it along until we get to it."

The other two nodded and we moved out.

A shot rang out behind me and I spun around to see Warrant holding his rifle. I followed the bead of his barrel and watched what looked like a bear slump against the staircase railing and then flip over it, landing on the ground below with a heavy thud. I lifted my rifle and kept an eye on the stairs. A shadow appeared at the top of the stairs.

Two hairy legs came into view and started to make their way down. Warrant hadn't put his rifle down and had it still aimed at the stairs. We waited to see what would appear. The creature came cautiously down but not cautiously enough. Warrant tagged it as soon as it showed its ugly head.

We waited a few minutes to see if anything else might try to come down but nothing did. We inched along the wall and kept our eyes on the stairs. Nothing moved. I guessed the doctor hadn't made it after all. But where was her body?

"Think there's more of them up there?" the sergeant asked.

"I think it's safe to say there probably are," I answered.

All three of us moved to the bottom of the stairs and looked up. We saw nothing but darkness.

"Where's the Doc?" the sergeant asked.

"We have to assume she's dead, most likely up there," I answered, still looking into the darkness above.

"I can't see a way to assault that top landing without taking a beating," Warrant said grimly.

"Well, we can't just stand here," I said.

"I have an idea," the sergeant said.

"Hope it's a good one," I answered back.

The sergeant walked towards a jeep parked a few yards from where we stood. "Look at the roof," he said, "there are searchlights mounted on top."

"Good thinking," Warrant cut in.

The sergeant and I looked at him in wonder, neither of us used to hearing anything positive coming from his mouth.

The three of us got to work quickly, always keeping an eye on the staircase for uninvited guests. We made short work of it and had something rigged up almost immediately from stuff found lying around in the hangar. We'd decided, since it had been the sergeant's idea, he could hold the light in place and beam it up the staircase as Warrant and I made our way up.

"See anything?" I asked.

"Nothing," Warrant replied.

The sergeant followed closely behind us keeping the light steady. Halfway up we stopped. The stairs ended onto a large landing that opened up on both sides. Our heads were just above the floor line when I thought I heard something.

"Flash the light over to our right," Warrant ordered, back to his old self again.

The sergeant lifted the light. The beam exposed a wall of boxes placed along the wall. We stood staring for a minute but nothing moved.

"Scan the rest of the area," Warrant said.

The landing looked like a dumping ground for unused materials. Upturned desks, chairs and old flags littered the place. At the end of the landing were metal doors that led to the control tower.

"It looks clear," I said.

Warrant and I inched up the stairs. Once on the landing, I expected a surprise attack but none came.

"Who wants the honors of announcing our arrival?" Warrant asked.

I stepped forward and was about to knock when boxes to our right began falling to the floor. All three of us spun around in time to see a figure appear from the shadows.

"Hit it with the light so we can get a clear shot," I said, trying to get a bead on whatever it was.

The beam of light cut across us and focused all its intensity on the figure of Doctor Slaughter who covered her eyes from the blinding light.

"Turn the light away, you idiot," she yelled.

Sarge lowered the spotlight as Warrant and I lowered our weapons.

"What the hell were you doing back there?" Warrant questioned. "Why didn't you say something when we came up?"

"I didn't know it was you," she said. "I've been hiding back there not knowing what was going on. I heard gunshots and then everything went quiet. I wasn't sure if any of you were still alive."

"How the hell did you get by the creatures?" the sergeant asked.

"They must have been down below when I came up," she answered. "I was about to knock on the door when I heard them coming up the stairs so I hid in the only place I could find."

Warrant and I looked at each other and I wondered if he was thinking the same thing as I. It seemed odd that she could have managed to get by them without being noticed but with everything I'd been through I guessed anything was possible.

I turned to the sergeant. "Sarge, go bang on the door and get them to open up.

CHApTER SIx

It surprised me to see how few people were in the tower. I don't know what I'd expected but it was certainly more than the six people who now stood in front of us wide-eyed and frightened.

"Thank God you've arrived," a woman wearing way too much make-up said to me.

"Where are the others?" a guy with a mechanics outfit asked. "We only saw the one chopper. Are the rest waiting for the all-clear?"

I took in the room. Everything still seemed operational. A good sign, I guessed. "We're all there is."

"That can't be," the woman spoke up.

"It can and it is," Warrant commented.

"Pipe down," I told Warrant. "Look everyone, we're all safe and that's what counts for the moment. I noticed everything still looks operational. Have you been in contact with anyone?"

An older guy with a pinched face spoke up. I guessed him to be a tech guy. "No," he answered.

"Are communications down?" I asked.

"General Ryan cut all communications after he found out the perimeter had been breached."

"Where's the General now?"

"He flew off with about a dozen others right before we were attacked."

The heavily made-up woman pushed herself through the group and approached me, tears beginning to smear her mascara. "They never even told us they were leaving," she sobbed.

"Slow down and take a breath," I suggested. "It's going to be okay." I didn't know if I believed that or not but it sounded right.

She looked at me with disbelief in her eyes. "It's going to be okay? Three men and a woman? You're our protection? There are hundreds of those things out there."

"They're all dead," I told her. "We checked the area when we came in. It's all clear."

"It's not all clear," she screamed at me. "Those things you see dead down there are only a handful of what attacked us."

"I know you're upset but I can assure you…"

The mechanic interrupted me. "It's true. We watched hundreds of them run into the forest just before you arrived. Half of them still had military clothing on from before they turned into those creatures."

I let that thought run through my mind. If they were out there why hadn't they attacked us when we were exposed in the field? I walked to the window of the tower and looked out. I could see the helicopter and could just make out the pilot having a smoke against its side. If those things were still out there, why weren't they attacking?

I ran different scenarios through my mind. If these things could communicate it meant they had some intelligence and if they were smart, the first thing they'd want to do would be to get reinforcements.

My eyes followed the tree line for movement. Nothing out of the ordinary caught my eye. Although deep in thought I could make out the arguing going on behind me. I tried to ignore them as I attempted to put myself in the creatures' heads. I guessed once they saw the General and the others take off, they realized the base was of no further use to them.

Then a horrible thought hit me.

The closest source for reinforcements would be in town. I spun around and faced the arguing group. "Stop it," I yelled. It surprised me how quickly they all shut up. "Listen to me. The creatures are gone. My guess is they're headed towards town. You," I said, pointing at the tech guy. "You're a technician, right?"

"Yes," he muttered.

"I want you to get communications back up, fast. We have to contact the town and warn them."

He didn't bother to respond but hustled away and grabbed some tools from a drawer across the room and got to work.

"Okay, first things first," I said. "Are any of you hurt?"

They all shook their heads.

"Good, then let's make some introductions so we know who one another are. I'm Cross, this is Major Warrant and Sergeant, I'm sorry Sarge, all this time and I have no idea what your name is."

"Saunders," the sergeant answered.

"And this is Sergeant Saunders," I informed them.

"I'm Megan," the woman with the caked-on make-up said. "I'm one of the air traffic controllers here." She looked towards the guy busy working on one of the consoles and said, "That's Randy, he's our resident techie."

"Pleasure to meet you, Megan," I said. "And you are?" I asked the guy with the mechanic's jumpsuit.

"Kirk, I'm one of the mechanics here. I work with Brian over there in the motor pool." Brian lifted his hand in a half wave.

I smiled at the two of them in hopes of looking confident about the situation. I turned to the last two and they seemed different from the others and much more nervous. "And who are you two?"

These two were a man and a woman. They looked like they could have been a couple but I wasn't sure. Neither of them answered. A look of fear or shock sat heavily on their faces.

"It's okay now, you're among friends," I offered.

Still no response. The room had grown strangely quiet and I turned around. Pointed right at me was the barrel of a gun. A gun held by Doctor Slaughter.

"What the hell are you doing?" I asked.

"Don't interfere," she said. "These two traitors are the ones who caused this problem."

"You lie," the woman screamed. "You're the one who caused all this." Before she could say another word a bullet entered her forehead and blew out the back of her head.

"Hey," I shouted in surprise, but before I could get another word out, the woman's friend charged at the Doctor.

The doctor squeezed off another round and hit him in the chest, knocking him to the floor. Warrant quickly disarmed the doctor while Sarge hung back with his weapon covering her.

"You'll be okay," I offered, as I knelt beside the dying man. "Just hang in there."

He said something but I couldn't make it out. I knelt closer to him and wiped the blood from his lips.

"Don't trust her," he whispered and coughed up more blood. He took a few deep breaths and through his spittle, he mumbled something I couldn't understand.

"What?" I asked.

He coughed up a large amount of blood. I tried my best to keep his mouth clear but the blood kept coming. He coughed again and looked at me. "Don't trust her, she communicates…" Those were his last words.

I pulled myself up and stormed toward the doctor. "What the hell do you think you're doing?" I yelled at her.

"Tell your goon to let me go," she said, struggling against Warrant's tight hold.

"Why? So you can shoot one of us? Tie her to a chair," I told Warrant.

"Gladly," he replied. He grabbed her roughly and dragged her fighting to a chair and began to tie her to it with Sarge's help.

The remaining survivors stared in horror at me.

"I'm sorry," I said, "I think it's time for us to get out of here. I need you all to pull yourselves together, okay."

None of them answered.

"Megan, Kirk and Bruce," I said, hoping I got their names right. "I need you to go find supplies. Anything you think we'd need for an extended trip. Food, weapons, water and something to carry them in. Got it?"

The three of them nodded.

"Good. Get to it. Sarge, go with them and keep them safe. I'll help Randy while Warrant keeps an eye on the doctor. Watch the time and be back within fifteen minutes."

The four of them left the room

"Did you pat her down?" I asked Warrant.

"She's clean," he said.

"You can't do this to me," she yelled as she struggled against her binds. "I'll have you both court-martialed."

"Gag her," I said.

Randy and I worked on the communication system until we had it up and running, at least partially. Slaughter had quieted down and just stared out the window as if she was trying to will herself to a different place. The four I'd sent out were back and Warrant helped them divide the stuff they'd found equally. I wasn't sure yet what I was going to do with the doctor but I'd worry about her later.

I looked out the window and noticed the sun coming up over the far horizon. I could feel the lack of sleep begin to kick in. I wanted to sit down and rest but knew the others were looking to Warrant, Sarge and I for strength.

"I've got something," Randy said.

The doctor began to struggle and mumble something through her gag. The rest of us ignored her and circled around Randy.

"What do you have?" I asked.

"Local authorities."

It wasn't the backup I'd hoped for. "No communications with the General or military?"

"No," Randy replied. "They fouled up the lines good before they left. It took me this long just to receive civilian communications. Even now we can only listen in. I haven't got it two-way yet."

"Can you pipe it through an intercom for us to hear?" I asked.

"Sorry, I..."

"That's fine," I told him. "What are you hearing?"

He listened into the headset again and seemed to be struggling to make out what he heard. Finally, he turned to us and said, "Doesn't sound like anything is happening. Everything sounds normal from the conversations I'm picking up."

"Are you sure?" Warrant asked. "Those creatures should have easily reached the town by now."

"Well, if they have, the town cops don't know anything about it," Randy said.

Sarge looked at me. "Could they be headed in another direction? Maybe back to Harmony?"

"Wouldn't make sense," I told him. "But it's the best news I've heard so far." I tried to put myself into the heads of the creatures again so I could try to guess what they might do next. Nothing added up. "Look everyone. I don't see a need to stay here any longer. I think our best bet is to get into town. They have food, clothing, shelter and communications there. If no one has a better idea, I say we move out."

"Look," Megan screamed. She stared out the window and had the look of someone who might have just seen a fiery meteor heading towards her. We turned to look. Streaming from the surrounding forests were dozens of creatures.

I couldn't see the pilot but the helicopter crawled with the creatures. Now our only way into town was through them.

"I need someone to go down and get one of the armored vehicles started," I said. "Our only chance is to mow our way through them."

"I'll do it," Kirk said.

"I'll go with him," Sarge added.

"Good, better get to it," I told them.

They left without another word.

Warrant stepped up. "You heard the man. Grab the supplies, pack up and get ready to go." As everyone grabbed their stuff he leaned into me. "What about her?" he asked nodding to Slaughter.

"We'll have to take her with us," I answered. "Untie her and warn her what'll happen if she doesn't cooperate."

"That's the spirit," he replied.

As I loaded my rifle and sidearm, I was tempted to put a bullet through Slaughter's forehead. After I finished rearming myself, I helped the others pack and made sure they each had a weapon of their own.

"You idiots," Slaughter called out, now ungagged. "You think you can make your way through all of them?"

I turned to her. "Have a better idea?"

She smiled at me. "I already have a plan but it doesn't include any of you."

"Sorry to rain on your parade, sister, but your plan is to shut the fuck up and to do as you're told," Warrant cut in.

"We'll see," she said.

I didn't bother to argue with her. Warrant and I checked everyone's packs and moved them out. We hit the stairs at a run as the sound of a heavy motor rumbled beneath us. We hustled down the stairs and saw the huge armored personnel carrier waiting. The back door stood open and Sarge waved us in. Everyone rushed in and grabbed a seat. Warrant slammed the door shut and we took off.

"Everyone sit tight," I said. "The ride might get a bit bumpy." I walked past the seated group and up to where Kirk sat. Through the screened window I could see the creatures advancing on our position. "Think we can get through them?" I asked.

"No problem," he answered. "This thing can go through a brick wall." He quickly drove out of the hangar.

The creatures didn't seem fazed at all as we approached and I worried they knew something we didn't.

The first wave hit us, rocking our vehicle from side to side.

"They're throwing themselves at us," Kirk said in disbelief.

"Can you get through them?"

"Shouldn't be a problem but I've never seen anything move a rig like this before." He seemed bewildered. "I don't know if it's the sheer number of them or if they have some kind of super-strength or both."

"Keep driving," I ordered.

A sudden gust of air blew against my back and shouting be-hind me caught my attention. I turned just in time to see the doctor hurl herself out the back door. I watched in disbelief as she tum-bled along the ground and disappeared out of sight. I rushed back and met with Warrant and Sarge who were struggling to close the door.

"What the hell happened?" I asked as I helped close the door.

"Beats the hell out of me. One second she was sitting there all docile, the next she had the door open and was gone," Warrant answered.

"We have to get her back," I said.

"Are you nuts? Good riddance if you ask me," Warrant re-plied.

"She's the only one we know who has any idea what these things are. We have to get her back."

"Shit."

I raced back to the front and told Kirk the good news. He looked at me as if I was out of my mind. I finally convinced him to turn it around and when he did, neither of us could believe our eyes. Slaughter stood in the middle of the creatures pointing this way and that as if she was their commander issuing orders. What seemed stranger was the fact they seemed to obey her.

"What the hell?" Kirk said as he slammed on the brakes.

"Back it up," I shouted, but it was too late. The pounding from our right side echoed through the vehicle. Before we even had a chance to back up, we tipped over and found ourselves helpless on our side.

I picked myself up and checked to see if everyone was all right. Except for bumps and bruises, everyone was uninjured.

"What now?" Warrant yelled to me over the screams of the creatures outside.

Sarge helped the others to their feet.

"Hell if I know," I answered.

The creatures' howls stopped and Doctor Slaughter's voice spoke to us. "Get out of the vehicle," she ordered.

Warrant and Sarge looked at me. I shrugged and held up my hand.

"Come out now," she bellowed. "If you don't, we'll burn you out."

"Bitch," Megan screamed.

Everything became silent.

I walked to the back door and called out. "Will we be safe if we come out?"

"Safer than if you stay in there," she replied. "You have one more minute to come out before we force you out."

"Why are you doing this?" I yelled.

"Because I can," she replied.

A minute hadn't even gone by before I began to smell the smoke.

"Open the door," I said resignedly.

The Sarge opened the hatch and we climbed out. The sun over the trees felt warm against my skin. I wondered if this was the last time I'd feel its warmth.

"Do you like my children?" Slaughter asked with a smirk. Creatures of all shapes and sizes surrounded her. There were creatures with fur, creatures with feathers, some with scales some beyond description.

"I see the family resemblance," Warrant told her.

"That's funny."

Warrant didn't reply.

"What are you doing?" I asked her. "What are you trying to gain from all this?"

"Revenge," she answered.

"On who?"

"Mankind, a stupid race of beings who didn't know a good thing when they had it."

I looked at the creatures around us. I knew there wasn't a hope of escape with their numbers. I thought again of my son and anger built up inside me. I knew then if I was about to go down I'd take her with me if Warrant didn't beat me to it.

"What are you planning to do?" I asked.

"Kill you, of course. You and your friend Warrant are everything that's wrong with society."

"What about the others? They've done nothing to you."

"You don't get it. They're all part of the rotten system. The whole lot of you."

Megan surprised us all by stepping forward. "And what about you? What makes you so different from us?"

"Vision," she said simply.

"How do you control them?" I asked the doctor.

"I don't control them," she answered. "We are one. They can think for themselves but we are all bound by common genetics."

"Yours, I'm guessing?"

"Exactly."

"So that's what you were doing up there at Harmony? Creating a new race based from your own DNA? Kind of self-centered, don't you think?"

"Enough talk," she said.

"One thing," I asked, not giving her time to reply. "Won't you be alone when no one else of your kind is left?"

"Don't be stupid. Do you think this could all be done by one person? You flatter me."

"The General?"

She laughed. "That idiot? He'd be the last one I'd bring into the family."

"Then who?"

"Others like me who believe as I do that we have to start over. As we speak, trucks are moving in every direction with members of my family to carry on the work."

"You're mad," Kirk called out.

"Perhaps but you won't live long enough to have to worry about it." She turned to her brood and without a word, sent them some kind of message.

They began to close in on us.

The sound of a chopper made everyone look to the sky. Out from behind the hangar rose an Apache gunship which immediately opened fire.

"Take cover," I yelled, as I ran back to our disabled vehicle.

The hissing of missiles filled the air. I helped usher everyone back into the vehicle and just managed to scramble in and close the door when the earth heaved beneath me. Warrant and Sarge held the door shut as the sound of howling and machine-gun fire rained down around us.

"Where the hell did that Apache come from?" Warrant asked.

"Beats me but they sure took their sweet time getting here."

Bullets and debris peppered our vehicle and I could tell everyone was scared. The pandemonium eventually quieted down until only the sound of the chopper's blades remained.

"Think it's safe to poke our heads out?" Sarge asked.

"Be my guest," I answered.

Sarge slowly opened the hatch and swung the door open. Dirt blew into the hold and we lifted our shirts over our mouths to keep it out. The Apache drifted from the sky and landed a few yards from us. I quickly looked around and saw the charred and mutilated bodies of the creatures strewn everywhere.

There was no sign of the Doctor.

Gunshots rang out and I turned to see Warrant taking shots at one of the creatures running into the forest. I looked around and noticed a few more creatures also disappearing into the forest. Was Slaughter among them?

"Come on," Warrant yelled over the din of the rotary blades.

I covered our escape as we ran towards the Apache. I grabbed a seat and wiped the perspiration off my face with my sleeve. I looked up to thank our pilot and got the surprise of my life. The pilot who'd saved us earlier had come through again. He gave me the thumbs-up as he lifted the bird into the air. I wanted to ask him how he'd managed it, but exhausted, I knew it'd have to wait.

Thoughts of my son filled my head as I drifted off to sleep.

CHAPTER SEVEN

The town was alive with activity as we walked its bustling sidewalks. Stores began to open their doors for the day as children crossed the streets on their way to school. Rush hour traffic snaked its way along the busy streets mingling with bikers and pedestrians.

"Think she was full of shit?" Warrant asked.

"I don't know," I answered. "You'd think they'd be here by now."

Sarge stood staring at the morning traffic before approaching us. "Maybe the chopper jockey nailed what was left of them."

"Could be," I said.

"You have to figure the army must have made a dent in them as well. How many of them could there be left?"

"I guess it depends on if you believed the Doc or not," I said.

Warrant grunted.

"What now?" Megan asked.

"I have to find my son," I answered.

"We have to tell people what's happening," she said.

"Do what you can," I said, "but find your families and try to keep them out of sight for a while. Who knows if those things are going to show up again?"

"Then what?" Kirk asked.

"I don't know."

Warrant surprised me by walking over and shaking my hand. Sarge did the same.

"Where are you two going?" I asked.

"I'll try to track down the General and find out where he needs us," Warrant told me. "If worse comes to worst, I'll go to the local authorities and fill them in."

"You think they'll show up during the day or wait for nightfall?" I asked.

"Who knows?" he replied, not seeming to care.

Megan rushed over to me and gave me a hug, but before I could say anything she broke off and darted across the street and disappeared around a corner.

"Guess I'll get going as well," Kirk said, shaking my hand. "Thanks for everything." He turned and shook hands with Warrant and Sarge and ran off down the sidewalk.

"I think it's over," Randy said. "Maybe I'll go get some breakfast."

"Mind if I join you?" Brian asked.

"Not at all."

We all shook hands and I watched as the two of them walked away and entered a diner up the street.

I turned to our pilot. "What about you?"

"I'll get the bird back in the air and see if I can spot anything in the surrounding areas. Maybe it is all over."

"I meant to ask you, how did you end up with the Apache?"

He looked at me with an embarrassed smile. "I know I was supposed to watch my chopper but I noticed the Apache sitting under some camouflage netting and just had to have a look."

I nodded, thanking God he had left his post. I shook his hand and turned to Sarge.

"Sure you don't want to stick with us?" Sarge asked me.

"I'm sure," I said. "I have to find my son and make sure he's safe. But look, if things turn bad let's pick a rendezvous point."

"Where?" Warrant asked.

I thought about it for a minute. "How about the clearing on top of Saddler's Hill?"

"Works for me," Sarge said.

"Fine," Warrant agreed.

"When exactly?" the pilot asked.

"If things turn ugly," I said, "make your way to the rendez-vous point. If you're not comfortable hanging around, come back every hour on the hour. If you move on, leave a note somewhere along the base of the boulder where the kids spray paint, letting us know you're alive and where you're headed."

We all agreed, shook hands and said our goodbyes. I stood alone on the sidewalk watching the others disappear into the early morning crowd until finally I turned and walked away myself.

CHAPTER EIGHT

I followed the crowds along the busy sidewalks as I headed toward my son's school. I still had no idea what I'd tell him or his teacher but at this point, I didn't see any benefit in telling my story unless I wanted to cause a panic. They'd probably think I was nuts anyway. No, I'd just say there was a family emergency.

I felt nervous wondering what Ben would say when he saw me. He'd know right away something was up. He was bright for his age but I guess every father thinks that way. I remembered the first time we'd gone on a family vacation. I'd brought Ben and Tara to Gettysburg to show him some history. We climbed Little Round Top and I showed them where Chamberlain had held the Union line and possibly saved the entire northern army.

Ben appeared to have a natural grasp for sizing up a battle-field. As we climbed the hill, he told me how he'd have never ordered his men up that embankment but would have instead taken Big Round Top and shelled the opposing hill with everything he had. My little general. As for the infamous Pickett's Charge, Ben decided, there was no way he'd have marched his men across that open field either. Instead, he would have tried a flanking maneuver on both ends of the Union line with hopes he could peel them back like a banana.

Of all our vacations I think that was my favorite. Ben and I re-ally managed to bond and for the first time, I began to see him as a young man instead of a little boy. It had been great weather and we'd spent most of the time outdoors, hiking around. On our last day, I took him to a store in town because he'd wanted a souvenir. After spending an hour browsing, he'd finally decided on a Civil War chess set. It cost me a pretty penny but it was worth it to see the smile on his face.

I wish I could have been a better father to him and that I could have been with him more but the strained relationship with Tara made it impossible. The thought brought a new problem to mind. What was I going to do about Tara? I'd have to warn her but I could only imagine what her reaction would be. I didn't know what was worse, going up against those creatures again or having to spend time with Tara.

The schoolyard bustled with children playing while they waited for the bell that signaled the start of class. As I approached, I scanned the yard looking for Ben but didn't see him. I looked around and didn't see any teachers either so I figured it was safe to enter the yard without being hassled. Before long I spotted him. A group of kids were kicking a soccer ball around towards the back of the schoolyard.

Ben spotted me before I had the chance to call his name. He ran over with a huge grin on his face.

"What are you doing here?" he asked.

"Came to pick you up so we could have a father and son day."

He looked at me suspiciously. "Is Mom okay?"

"Yes, she's fine."

"She didn't tell me you were dropping by to pick me up."

"It was a last-minute thing. I forgot I had today off."

He looked like he was trying to read my thoughts. "So where are we going?"

"Don't know yet but let's head out before the bell rings."

One of the kids he'd been playing with walked towards us with the soccer ball. "Hey Ben," he called out. "You playing?"

"No," he answered. "I'm taking off. You guys go ahead."

His friend just waved and punted the ball back towards the others and ran after it.

As Ben and I walked through the yard he looked up at me. "You going to tell me now what's up?"

"You're turning out to be just like your mother," I told him. "Always suspicious."

We left the schoolyard just as the bell rang. On the sidewalk we headed west toward the house where he and Tara lived, the house I'd once called home.

"Where's your truck?" he asked.

"Back at my place. A buddy let me off and I walked over to the school."

He gave me another of those questioning looks.

I felt bad keeping him in the dark but decided it would be better to explain it all to him once we were safely off the street.

"Where we headed?" he asked.

"We'll go to your place first and pick up a few things."

"Like what?"

"Some camping gear, maybe."

That brought a smile to his face. "Are you serious?" he asked. "Are we really going camping?"

"Only if you want to."

"All right. Will it be an overnight?"

"Possibly."

"Come on, tell me."

"Okay, you guessed it. It's an overnight."

"And Mom okayed it?"

"Of course," I lied. "I've been planning this for a while."

We continued our walk making small talk and laughing and just enjoying each other's company.

"Guess what?" he said.

"What?"

"Mom and I think we saw an alien last night."

My heart just about stopped. "What?"

"I think Mom and I saw an alien last night," he repeated.

"What kind of an alien?"

"It was all silver or gray," he told me. "I'm not too sure because it was pretty dark. I looked out my bedroom window before I shut the blinds and it was standing in the back yard."

I couldn't believe what I was hearing. "What did it look like?"

"Like I said, it was silver or gray. It kind of looked like a snake but it had hands and feet like a man."

"Did it see you?"

"I don't think so."

"What was it doing?"

He thought about it for a second before answering. "It wasn't really doing anything. It just kind of stared up into the sky as if it was waiting for something."

"And your Mom saw it too?"

"Yeah, I called her up to come take a look."

"What did she do when she saw it?"

"She started screaming," he answered. "Girls."

"Did it hear her?"

"I think so because it took off."

I thought about this new information and wondered what it meant. Obviously they were in the city somewhere. Or maybe it was just a scout sizing up the situation. Either way, they were here.

Tara kept the small townhouse as tidy as I remembered. Newspapers and magazines littered the floor and tables. Dishes overflowed in the sink.

"Don't you help out around here?" I asked.

Ben shrugged.

"Go get packed," I told him. "I'll call your mother while you're getting ready."

Ben raced up the stairs to his bedroom and I could hear him rifling through his closet and drawers. I threw some papers off a chair and dropped myself into the recliner. I ran my hands through my hair and wondered what I'd tell her when I called. I studied the phone beside me on the end table and finally picked it up.

The phone rang twice before she answered it. "Destiny Travel," she said.

"Hi Tara, it's James."

Nothing but silence answered me.

"You there?"

"What do you want?" She asked.

"I need you to come home," I told her. "I'm with Ben at your place and we have to talk."

More silence.

"You there?"

"I want you out of my house."

"Listen, Tara, this is important."

"What kind of trouble are you in?"

"I'm not in any trouble," I told her. "I just need to talk to you."

I heard her say something to someone else in her office. I lifted a magazine on psychic healing and shook my head. She came back on the line. "Some people were here waiting for me this morning when I arrived. They wanted to know if I'd seen you."

"What kind of people?"

"They looked military but were in civilian clothes," she said. "What kind of trouble are you in?"

"I can't talk over the phone. Please come home."

"I can't. I have work to do and I can't just take off any old time I want."

"It's important."

"I bet it is," she said. "I want you to get out of my house and take Ben back to school. Who the hell do you think you are taking him out without my permission?"

"His father."

She didn't say anything at first, then she warned me, "If you don't get out I'm calling the cops and the MPs."

I raced through my options and with nothing to lose I said, "That thing you saw last night with Ben. They're not aliens, there's a lot more of them and they're on their way."

"Don't try to play me for a fool."

"It's not a joke," I said. "Okay, look, I have an idea. Hang up and call the base and try to find someone who knows where I am."

"What's that going to prove?"

"Just do it," I told her. "If you call back and you still don't want to come over, I'll bring Ben back to school and won't bother you again."

The phone went dead. I hoped she was calling the base and not the authorities. Unable to just sit there and wait I pulled myself from the recliner and walked to the foot of the stairs. "How are you doing up there?" I yelled.

"Good," he answered.

I walked to the kitchen and looked at the mess that surrounded me and hoped I could find a clean glass. I did and filled it with water and took a sip. The phone rang on my third sip and I hustled to the phone. "Hello?"

"No one's answering," Tara said.

"Did you let it ring?"

"Of course."

"Have you ever called the base and not had someone answer before?"

"What's going on? You're scaring me."

"Just come home." I paused. "Please?"

"Dad," Ben screamed from upstairs.

"Hang on," I said to Tara. I dropped the phone and sprinted to the stairs. "You all right?" I shouted up at Ben.

"There's something in the back yard."

I ran up the stairs and into Ben's room. He stood staring out the window. I walked to the window and looked out. Staring up at us were four of the same kind of creatures I'd come across last night. "Do you have a phone up here?" I asked Ben.

"Yeah, over there." He pointed at his dresser.

"Keep an eye on them and tell me if they move." I went to the phone and snatched the receiver from its cradle. "You still there?" I asked into it.

"What's going on there?" Tara asked.

"No time to explain," I said. "Listen, don't come here. We'll come there. Don't leave the building until I show up."

"James, tell me what's going on."

"Just do what I told you. We'll be there soon. I have to go." I didn't give her a chance to say anything more because I knew we'd never get off the phone. I hung up the phone and raced back to the window. They were still there.

"What do you think they're doing?" Ben asked me.

"I have no idea. Stay here and yell if they move. I have to get something and I'll be right back."

I left the bedroom and hustled down the stairs and into the family room. I grabbed my duffel bag and ran back upstairs. I threw the bag on the bed, opened it up and pulled out my rifle. Ben stared at me with wide eyes. "It's okay," I tried to reassure him. I grabbed some ammo and loaded the rifle.

"You going to shoot them?" he asked me.

"Do you have all your stuff together?"

"Yeah."

"Good. Look, I need you to go and grab some stuff for Mom. She's going to be coming with us."

"Really?"

"Yes, now get going."

The creatures stood in the backyard as if they were in a trance. None of them moved. I wondered if there were more of them around. Out front maybe? "Ben, you grabbing that stuff?"

Ben yelled back from the other room. "Yeah, almost done."

"Hurry it up and get back in here."

Ben entered the room not long after and tossed his bag on the bed. "I'm scared," he said.

"It's going to be okay."

Ben didn't look too sure.

"Now listen to me. It's going to be okay. We're going to go downstairs now and walk out the front door if the coast is clear. If everything looks okay we'll walk to your Mother's work and pick her up."

"Why don't we take her car?" he asked. "It's just sitting in the garage."

"How'd your Mom get to work?"

Ben didn't answer and looked down at his feet.

"Come on Ben we don't have time for games."

"Her boyfriend drove her," he said, his eyes still focused on his feet. "They went for breakfast."

It was the first time I'd heard anything about a boyfriend but I couldn't worry about it now. "Okay fine, we'll head for the garage and take the car."

"You're not mad?"

"No, I'm not mad," I told him. To be honest I didn't know what I felt. "Come on let's go."

CHAPTER NINE

We sat in the car in the garage. I felt hesitant to break the silence by starting the engine. For the first time since the whole thing began I actually felt safe. I knew it was a false sense of security because outside of our little cocoon, a world gone mad was waiting for us.

"Are we going to go get Mom?" Ben asked, breaking me from my thoughts.

I turned and looked at him but it only made me want to stay there longer. I shook it off and forced a smile to spread across my face. "Yep."

I started the car and let it idle for a bit. The thought of staying put and letting the carbon monoxide do its trick occurred to me but I knew I'd never be able to do it. I put my foot on the brake, shifted the car into drive and unclipped the garage door opener from the visor. I played with it for a second until finally I pressed it.

The door shuddered and began to open. I held my breath as the door creaked open. "Hold tight," I told Ben, "I may have to do some fancy driving."

Ben nodded and I checked to make sure he had his seat belt on.

The light from outside filled the garage and to my relief, there wasn't a soul to be seen. I stepped on the gas and shot out of the garage. I hung a left at the end of the driveway and was surprised to see how empty the street was. I eased up on the gas pedal and drove towards downtown, only a ten-minute drive away, to where Tara worked.

Elm and maple trees lined the street. Everything seemed so normal. I missed the neighborhood and began to resent Tara for what she'd done to our family. I turned left again at an intersection and still, there was no one around.

"You okay?" I asked Ben who'd been awfully quiet.

"Where is everyone?" he asked.

"I don't know."

The sound of a shot rang out. I slammed on the brakes. As the car came to a halt a second shot sounded. It sounded like it was coming from the downtown area.

"Are those guns?" Ben asked, wide-eyed.

"Shhh," I said, holding a finger to my lips. A third shot rang out and I counted. The next shot came approximately three seconds later. The next shot came three seconds after that and then there was nothing but quiet.

"He's moving position," I said under my breath.

"What?" Ben asked.

"Nothing," I said. "Sit tight."

I hit the gas and raced towards where I thought the shooting had come from. I recognized the sound of Warrant's shooting style and weapon. I was surprised, even with his reckless style, that he'd shoot five rounds before moving positions. Every sniper knew you waited for your best shooting option before firing because once you've made your shot you had to move so not to be discovered.

As we turned the next corner something out of the corner of my eye caught my attention. Before I could react something hit the windshield hard and sent a spider web of cracks across it. I swerved to the left and pressed harder on the gas pedal. Who had thrown that thing at us?

Up the street I noticed creatures emerging from homes with regular people calmly walking in front of them.

Out of nowhere the Apache appeared and thundered over us, disappearing behind buildings to our right.

My mind raced. What the hell was happening? Other than the brick or rock that was thrown at our car, no one else seemed to pay attention to us. We turned right onto the next street hoping to follow the Apache and found the same thing. People lined the sidewalks, escorted by those creatures. They all seemed headed in the same direction.

I turned onto Main Street which lead directly into the downtown core and was shocked to see it lined with row after row of people. Each of the lines faced downtown as they shuffled forward.

"What's going on," Ben asked.

"I don't know."

"Look at all the aliens," he continued. "Are they friendly?"

I didn't answer. My mind tried desperately to come up with a plan. It bothered me that none of the creatures tried to stop us. It was as if they were allowing us to continue unabated. I wondered if Slaughter had anything to do with it?

Up ahead, we saw the hockey arena and I noticed the lines of people entering it.

"Mom!" Ben yelled.

I turned my head just in time to see Tara entering the arena.

"What's she doing?" Ben asked.

"I don't know," I said as I pressed my foot harder on the accelerator.

Ben pressed his face and hands against the side window and stared in the direction of his mother. "But we can't leave her there. You have to go get her," Ben pleaded.

Despite our differences, I wanted to help Tara but there were just too many of the creatures around. I decided it was time to get out of town so we could warn others and get help. "There's too many creatures," I said, "we'll come back for her later."

We passed the arena, leaving Tara behind, and were about to turn towards the highway.

"Look," Ben cried out.

I'd already spotted them and slammed on the brakes. I looked around for a way out but there didn't seem to be one. The creatures had come out of nowhere and now had us boxed in on all sides.

"Dad?"

"Lock your door," I told him, which he did quickly. The thought of plowing through them occurred to me but their numbers were multiplying quickly. Chances were we'd only get bogged down in them. I cursed myself for not having my truck.

The creatures stopped approaching us. We were surrounded as they stood perfectly still, watching us.

Ben grabbed my arm. "What do they want?" he asked.

"I don't know."

"Will they hurt us?"

"No," I lied.

Ben pointed to the front of our car. "Look."

I turned and noticed the creatures parting, forming an open lane. Was it meant for us? Were they allowing us to leave or was it a trick?

As I studied them, trying to decide what to do, the decision was made for me. From the open lane, Slaughter appeared and slowly walked towards us. She showed no expression as she passed through the open lane which the creatures filled back in behind her.

We stared at each other through the windshield.

"Who's that?" Ben asked.

"A crazy lady," I told him.

She took three steps towards us and stopped. She stood alone. "Get out of the car," she ordered.

I put my hand on Ben's lap. "Don't move," I told him.

"Get out of the car," she said again.

Neither Ben nor I moved.

"Are we going to have to go through this again?" she asked.

I revved my car and thought I saw a look of uncertainty on her face. She took half a step back and stopped. I took my foot off the gas and opened my side window a crack. "What do you want?" I called out.

She took a step closer and stopped. "I want you to join us."

"We have no interest in joining you."

"We are the future," she said. "We are one with each other. Each knowing what the others are thinking. There will be no more wars, no more crime."

"And no more free will," I said.

"Progress comes with a price."

I shifted in my seat as my fingers tapped on the steering wheel.

A glint of light hit my left eye but before I could raise a hand it disappeared. The same glint of light appeared again and just as quickly disappeared. This annoyance repeated two more times before I realized it was Warrant. He was signaling for the kill shot. I instinctively wanted to locate where he was but knew that if I drew attention to him he'd most likely become trapped himself.

I thought about it for a moment and realized that if he'd had a clear shot he'd have taken it. He must be signaling for me to get her out into the open. I didn't like the idea of being bait while I was with my son but I saw no other option.

"I'm getting out to talk but my son stays in the car."

Slaughter smiled. "Sure."

I turned to Ben. "Stay put," I told him. "If anything happens to me, jump into the driver's seat and step on the gas pedal and drive right through them."

"Don't leave," he pleaded.

"I'll be right outside," I told him. "Everything will be fine." I leaned over and hugged him. "You're a good boy and I've always been very proud of you."

Ben began to cry and I felt a wave of anger build inside of me. I thought back about my last mission and the boy who'd finished my career. If I hadn't been able to complete my mission then would I be able to do what was necessary for Ben if the time came?

"Be right back," I finally said. I swung the door open and got out of the car. I left the door open. "Come towards me," I told her.

She took a few steps towards me. "It's not so bad you know." She took another step. "You must have realized by now that I allowed you to get this far. I wanted to show you how orderly everything was and how no one was being hurt or mistreated.

"Until they go in there," I said, pointing towards the arena.

"I assure you it's almost painless," she said.

"What, to be under your control?"

"Don't be so simple."

The sound of breaking glass made me spin around. Slaughter laughed at the sight of my son being dragged from the car by some half-human, half boar-like creature. "Stop it," I yelled.

Her laughing stopped. "Will you do as I say?"

I stared at my son being held by the creature and then back at her and in defeat said, "Yes."

"Go to your son," she said.

I rushed to Ben but as I reached out for him the creature sneered at me and lifted him over his head. I turned towards Slaughter. "What is this?" I asked.

"You're so simple," she said. "Did you think you could call the shots? This is the new world and I'm the one calling..." Before she could finish her sentence a bullet ripped through the back of her head, leaving a gaping hole where her face once was. I stared as her body swayed in place until finally dropping to her knees and then to the ground.

"Dad."

I turned towards my son and watched as he fell to the ground. The creature which had been holding him dropped to the ground as if in pain. I rushed to Ben, scooped him up and quickly backed away. As we reached the car I noticed all the other creatures were also on the ground.

My mind raced but I decided there was no safe way to drive through them. I reached in and grabbed my bag from the car. I took Ben's hand and the two of us ran as fast as we could through the writhing creatures.

I hoped wherever Warrant was, he had us covered. As we maneuvered through the creatures, I wondered if that was all it took to destroy them. Kill the brain and you killed the body?

Could it be that easy? I doubted it.

We broke through the mass of bodies and finally found some open pavement. I looked down at Ben and knew that I'd never let him out of my sight again.

Ben tugged at my arm. "What about Mom?"

I slowed down to a walk and finally stopped. In all the mayhem I'd forgotten about Tara. I wondered if it would be safe to go back? What if they got up again? I turned to face the arena and noticed the creatures were all still down. It might be safe. I took the first hesitant step forward when the doors to the arena burst open and people, normal people, came streaming out.

A feeling of jubilation washed over me.

I looked back to see if there was any sign of Warrant but there wasn't. I didn't relish the thought of having to walk through those creatures again and decided if I didn't have someone to watch over Ben I wouldn't risk it. "Can you see her?" I asked.

Ben lifted himself on his tiptoes and craned his neck to see. "Not yet."

A low unearthly groan emanated from ahead of us and I noticed the creatures were starting to stir. "Get back," I told Ben. We slowly backed up until I noticed a creature stagger to its feet. "Run," I yelled. Ben and I took off down the street as fast as we could run. We only got a few blocks before the screaming started. "Don't look back" I said. "Keep running."

I looked back however and to my horror saw that most of the creatures were getting back to their feet.

People continued to stream from the arena. Mingled with them now were newly transformed creatures. The scene became chaotic as the creatures attacked and dragged people to the ground.

The screams became louder.

I knew from experience that some of those creatures were incredibly fast and I realized our few blocks lead would never be enough.

The sound of a gunshot rang out, then another and another. I looked over my shoulder and saw creatures who'd been following us collapse to the ground.

Four more creatures appeared out of nowhere. They seemed to be some sort of wolf hybrid. They were gaining fast when a bullet took the first one down, literally decapitating it as it ran. The other three didn't slow down but continued on. A second shot sounded and spun one of the wolf creatures in midair until it dropped dead to the ground. The two others split up but didn't retreat.

"I can't run anymore," Ben told me

Had the moment finally come? Could I pull the trigger if I had to? The thought of my son becoming one of those things made me sick.

The screams from the crowd reached a fevered pitch. I threw my bag to the ground and wrenched out my rifle. "Get behind me," I told Ben. I took a bead on the closest creature and blew off its head. As I turned to find the second creature a shot rang out from behind us and beat me to it. I watched the wolf thing collapse in a heap, its chest heaving twice before it drew its last breath.

I swung the rifle over my shoulder and picked up the bag. "Let's go," I said. We hustled away as screams filled the air. I looked at Ben and saw tears streaming down his face. I wanted to comfort him as a father should but there was no time.

Ahead of us, a figure emerged from a building. Ben and I slowed our pace until I recognized Warrant.

"We're completely cut off," he said as he hustled over.

"Are you sure?"

"Yep," he said. "I had a bird's eye view from the building over there," he pointed to a hotel down the street, "and had a great vantage point. They're everywhere." He looked down at Ben. "You've grown since the last time I saw you."

I stared at him in amazement.

Ben just shrugged.

"Any word from the General?" I asked.

"I terminated him a few hours ago," he said. "He'd turned."

"Sarge?"

He just shook his head.

"Damn," was all I could manage. Then I remembered. "The bird's still in the sky," I told him. "He flew over us a while ago."

"Did he see you?" Warrant asked.

"Don't know," I said.

"I found a TV at the hotel so I flipped it to the news to see what was happening."

"And?" I asked.

"They're all over," he said. "All containment measures have failed."

"Options?" I asked.

"Slim to none and I think I just made it worse."

"How's that?" I asked.

"I thought that by killing the bitch it'd sever the connection with those things and maybe stop them. Looks like I was wrong."

A loud moan echoed off the buildings around us.

"It looks like she was the only thing keeping them under control. Now they're just like rabid animals." He pointed towards the arena. "Look at them, they're even attacking each other now."

Another moan, this time closer, filled the air around us.

"We have to find high ground," I said.

"You thinking of making a stand?"

"Without her, they have no plan," I said. "I don't think they even have any reasoning ability. If we build ourselves a sniper's nest, we can pick them off at will without giving up our location."

Warrant looked like he was thinking it over when he said, "What about the St. James?"

"That'll work," I said.

"I checked it out earlier," Warrant said. "It's out on a bluff and faces directly into the city. If we take a top floor, we should be sitting pretty."

Another moan caught our attention. This time from behind us. The three of us turned, only to see a bunch of those creatures cutting off our path to the St. James Hotel. Another louder moan drifted from around the corner of the arena. Within seconds a second group of creatures appeared. They were all around us.

Ben hugged my leg as if trying to disappear into me.

"Let's lock and load," Warrant said.

I checked my rifle and looked at Warrant. Warrant had a handgun in his hand as well. Warrant looked at me and then at Ben.

"Not yet," I said glumly.

We checked our weapons and readied our ammo and prepared ourselves. "Stay between us," I told Ben.

"Okay," he answered.

I looked through my scope and saw her almost right away. Or at least what she'd become. Tara stood in front of the second pack of the creatures by the arena. Some kind of malformed beak protruded from her face and feathers had sprouted generously over her body, leaving her clothes in tatters. I lowered my rifle to try to make her out with my naked eye but she was too far away, which pleased me. I wanted to make sure Ben never saw her like that.

I lifted my rifle back into place and aimed for Tara's head, just above her beak. I played with the trigger, finding it harder than I thought it would be. I took a breath, held it and fired. Tara went down as painlessly as I could make it.

"Here comes more of them," Warrant warned me.

I heard Ben whimper behind me.

A new sound suddenly filled my ears. The whoop, whoop, whoop of chopper blades from somewhere overhead. I looked up but only saw a shadow of it between some buildings off to my right.

A high-pitched hiss filled the air and then a pop. "Hit the ground," I yelled. I dragged Ben down and covered him with my body.

An explosion rocked the street we were on, throwing us around like sailors on a stormy sea. One after another, explosions exploded around us. I could feel the intense heat blow over me as I lay there covering Ben.

"You okay?" I yelled to Ben over the sound of the explosions. I couldn't make out what he said.

The explosions finally stopped and I looked up. Smoke, dust and debris filled the street. I heard the helicopter above us slowly coming down. The smoke swirled around us, lifting dirt and debris into our faces. I lifted Ben to his feet and looked over at Warrant as he attempted to clear the dust off of himself.

I recognized the chopper right away. "That jockey's got nine lives," I yelled to Warrant.

The chopper landed and the three of us sprinted for the hatch. I pushed Ben in and then hopped in myself. I half expected Warrant to salute and run off into the smoke, to carry on, but I imagine even he'd had enough because he scrambled into the helicopter right after me.

We lifted off the ground and hovered for a while until the smoke from the swirling blades cleared and we had a better view. Almost all of the creatures who'd surrounded us were dead.

The chopper veered away and our vantage point changed so I looked out my window and saw thousands more of the creatures streaming through the streets below.

As we skimmed the city's skyline, I held Ben's hand as he leaned his head against my side. I looked again out the window and the creatures below were fighting amongst themselves. Would we be able to use that to our advantage in the future, I wondered? Would there even be a future?

The chopper banked away from the downtown core and flew west. I had no idea where we were headed so I decided not to worry about it for now. I slid closer to Ben and put my arm around him. As we eased back against the bulkhead, I wondered how many days we had left together.

ACKNOWLEDGEMENTS

A special thanks to Michael Shotter, my partner on our podcast, *The Post Mortem Report* for his support and friendship.

And to Tanya Sprowl for all her great book cover designs.

ABOUT THE AUTHOR

Ronald McGillvray is a writer from Ottawa, Canada. He's published short stories, scripts, novellas and his most recent novel *Cutter's Deep*. He is currently working on a new novel which will be out soon. His horror short story collection, *Tales From The Parkland* is available as a print or ebook. His children's fantasy novella, James' *Journey To Dreamland* is also available as a print or ebook. His writing credits include the short story, *The Garbage Collectors*, which was published in *Horror Library Volume 2* as well as in their best of anthology. An audio version of his story, *Big Boy*, was produced by *Pseudopod*.

Two of his film scripts, *The Storm* and *The Goodbye*, were produced by Cellardweller Projects. The Storm was chosen as one of the films to be screened at the World Horror Convention. It also screened at the Shocklines Film Festival in New York City.

His story, *Head Case*, was made into a film produced by Columbia College in Chicago. His film script, *Magic Man*, was optioned by Hyde Park Media.

His stage play, *The Line*, was chosen as part of the reading series by the Saint John Theatre Company.

Find out more about Ronald McGillvray at RonaldMcGillvray.com.

Printed in Great Britain
by Amazon

55583695R00118